THE
BARRED
ROAD

by Adèle De Leeuw

THE
BARRED
ROAD

THE MACMILLAN COMPANY, *New York*

The Macmillan Company, New York
Collier-Macmillan Canada, Ltd., Toronto, Ontario

Printed in the United States of America

The verses of "A Legend," arranged by
Katherine Davis to the music of P. Tschaikowsky,
are from the Hollis Dann Music Series #4,
published by The American Book Company.

THE
BARRED
ROAD

1.

"Sue!"

The red sweater with the plaid skirt, or the blue one with the gray worsted? "Present!" she shouted back to her mother, her voice laughing.

"It's seven-thirty. Are you up?"

"*And* in my right mind," Susan Trowbridge answered. "Be down in a sec." The red sweater was due for a laundering; that settled that.

"Your breakfast will get cold."

"All right, I'll eat it raw." Pin back her hair; a dusting of powder on her snub nose, a fresh handkerchief; change purse. Scarf? No, not today. Books—oh, where was that Selected Reading List? Pen—darn, it was leaking again; she'd have to buy a new ball point one—

"Hey, Sis, lend me a quarter?"

Her brother's pert, scrubbed face appeared in the doorway, his eyes merry, his hair slicked down except for the one cow-lick that defied brushing.

"What makes you think I have a quarter?"

"You have a change purse."

"That doesn't mean it has anything in it . . . for you," she grinned at him to soften the blow.

"Oh well, I just thought I'd ask. You certainly hang onto your money."

"It's more than you do, you little spendthrift!" she retorted. "What *do* you do with yours?"

"Well, gosh," Kenny said at once, "how can you make fifty cents a week cover everything you want?"

"You can't. You just have to decide what's most important. . . . Here, I can spare a dime. I'm feeling softhearted early in the morning." He took it quickly and she said, "But I'll want it back, with interest!"

"Oh, sure, you won't let me forget. Thanks!"

She reached out to flatten his cow-lick and he ducked expertly. Together they clattered down the stairs.

Mr. Trowbridge looked up from his paper. A smile spread over his broad, pleasant face. "Well, well, haven't seen you since last night! You're a welcome sight after all the bad news in the paper."

His wife came from the kitchen, pushing back her thick brown hair. "Why do you read it, Henry? It will just upset your digestion."

"Nothing would upset my digestion, my dear, after those wheatcakes of yours."

"Is that a compliment?"

He laughed. "I admit I put it badly. What I meant was, I'm in such a good humor after your delicious cooking that nothing could disturb me, not even the state of the world."

"That's better . . . Kenny, have you washed—"

"Yes'm."

"You're so quick to answer, I wonder—Why, yes, you have. That's fine. . . . How do you want your egg, Sue?"

"No egg for me, Mom," Kenny said, spreading two slices of bread simultaneously with thick butter.

"I didn't ask you, young man. Sue?"

"Oh, scrambled, scrambled, or scrambled," she said blithely. "Just so it's scrambled."

"I thought so," her mother sighed. "Kenny, after breakfast, I'd like you to go out and pick up the papers in the yard. It's disgraceful—"

"Oh gosh, Mom, I picked 'em up last night!"

"Not these," his mother said, tightening her lips. "Those Garritys! Fine neighbors they are. . . . The place looks like a pigsty. And they must have had another party last night. There was such talking and laughing and loud radio music I couldn't sleep."

"I didn't hear them," her husband said mildly.

"Oh, you wouldn't. You were dead to the world in ten minutes. I just lay awake and fretted. . . . And then to

see the yard littered again with papers this morning—
They brought out a whole load of them yesterday, clearing
up the house for the party, I suppose, though they never
seem to do it otherwise, and then just laid them on the
back porch without anything to hold them down and the
wind blew them all over here, of course. Kenny—"

"But, Mom, there won't be any time!" he protested.

"You should get up when I call you and there would be
time."

"I'll help," Susan volunteered. She knew how the unsightly garden bothered her mother, and the Garritys *were*
hard to take sometimes. The old house seemed to spill over
with them; there were five children of assorted sizes; and
innumerable relatives, some with *their* children, were
always coming or going, spending a day or two, often a
week. They made a lot of noise, but they did have a good
time. The house was in constant need of repair, and was
never repaired. If a brick came loose on the stoop, it remained loose. If a board fell off the back porch, no one put
it back. A torn blind, a fallen window curtain, stayed that
way for weeks. It got on Mrs. Trowbridge's nerves. She
felt that the house reflected on the neighborhood, and she
tried to keep her own home spotless in contrast.

"Listen, Mom," Kenny said with a glitter in his eye,
"how about me picking up all their old papers and dump-
ing 'em on their back porch again?"

"You pick them up, and burn them . . . *right here*,"
Laura Trowbridge said firmly.

"Well, I think it's a good idea," he persisted. "Why
should we do their work for 'em? Now if I was—"

"Were," said his mother automatically. "And what's more, if you were a little older, perhaps you wouldn't have such silly ideas."

Sue heard the family argument, but with only half an ear. She was thinking happily, In spite of the Garritys, I'm glad we moved to Brookhaven. It's much nicer than Warren . . . and I'm going to like it at High. She liked it now. She fitted in. It was amazing how quickly she had adjusted and found a place for herself. They had been in town only a few months; she had gone to High just since the opening of school, six weeks ago. And yet already she had friends, she was part of a crowd, people were asking her to do things.

Only last week she had been made co-chairman of the Junior-Freshman Hop. It was a big job, and she was proud to have been chosen. The crowd kidded her. . . . "You'll be sorry!" . . . "That's what you get for sticking your neck out and saying you'd be glad to help!" . . . "I wouldn't be in your loafers for anything!" But it was just a form of friendly envy; it was their way of complimenting her.

Even in these few days she was full of plans, eager to get started. It would be fun working with her co, Dave. David Grinnell was one of the nicest boys at High. She thought, I'd even say *the* nicest, but I don't know them all. She must remember to make a date with him to talk things over; they'd have to get going if they wanted to make this super-special, and of course it had to be. Should she ask him up to the house? Or perhaps they could hash matters over down at the Coke Shop.

Kenny grumbled, "I bet I've stooped ninety-eight times!"

"Good for you! You'd do the same in gym and think nothing of it. Breathe in deep!" she teased him. "One, bend, two, rise, one, bend—"

"Talk to yourself," he muttered, stooping once more, and flinging a page of newsprint into a basket. "In gym we do it to music!"

"All right," she laughed. "I'll whistle while you work, how's that?"

"Why doesn't the wind blow the other way for a change? . . . Gosh, Sue, I'm going to be late to school!"

"Well, run along. It looks pretty good for the moment, and there'll probably be more by night anyhow."

He tore off without a backward glance, and Sue carried the basket into the garage, pausing to pick up a few stray scraps as she went. She'd have to hustle herself. But nothing could disturb her this morning. It was such a beautiful morning, and she felt happy inside.

She looked up through the branches of the old apple tree to the deep blue sky. In the mellow autumn light the house had a pleasant air, like a homely old friend. It wasn't a handsome house, not even a good-looking one, according to her mother's standards. She hadn't wanted to take it, but when they had moved to Brookhaven, it was one of the few available at the price they could afford. And it *was* well-built—or so the agent had said. But by now they had discovered that there were a great many things that needed looking after . . . old houses, however well-built, had to be kept up.

Her mother begrudged every dollar that was spent on it. She did not want to remain in this part of town particularly. It wasn't fashionable any more; it wasn't even in the so-called 'better section.' Years ago it had been; but the older families had moved away or built new homes on Indian Hill; the bigger houses, many of them, had been converted into two-family apartments, and business had crept up from town, encroaching block by block in this older residential section.

It didn't matter much to Sue. She liked the spaciousness of the house, the chance for each of them to have his own room, the neglected garden with its aromatic bushes and old trees. But her mother saw the work to be done to keep it in condition, the care of the garden—aggravated now by the untidy Garritys next door—and the fact that it was not an address of which she could be proud.

It was queer, Sue thought as she walked under the arching trees and scuffed happily in the drifts of gold and russet leaves. Her mother wasn't ambitious for herself so much as for them. She was always saying that she wanted 'the best' for them. By that, Sue realized, she meant nice clothes and good times, the proper social life, moving in what she considered the proper social circles. That was why she herself wanted to get 'into things'—the women's clubs, the church affairs, and to have a home in 'the better neighborhood.'

Brookhaven was a good town to live in, but it had its social strata, and Laura Trowbridge felt that it was important to be in one of the upper ones. As they had been in Warren.

"A dillar, a dollar, a ten o'clock scholar—" a deep voice said beside her, and Sue's heart gave a pleasant leap.

"Same to you, Dave."

He took her books with an easy gesture. "You look reluctant, to say the least."

"It's much too nice a day to go in," she confessed. "But it wasn't that. I was—ahem—thinking." She made it sound pompous.

A nice thing about Dave was that he could take you up quickly. "May I ask," he inquired with equal pomposity, "what was engaging your cerebration? Is that right? Well, anyhow, mentality?"

Brookhaven High loomed ahead of them, its wide wings of rosy brick, its windows glittering in the light. The flag whipped in the breeze from a tall pole set at the end of the converging walks, and groups of students were sauntering toward the white doors.

"I was thinking," Sue improvised hurriedly, "that we'd better hump ourselves on plans for the Hop."

"Yea, verily," David agreed. "How about beating our brains out over a couple of cokes tomorrow?"

"Swell." That was settled, then. He could come to the house later. He had asked *her* . . . the happy feeling inside increased.

"Oops! There goes warning bell. Race you!"

His long legs sprinted ahead. She panted behind him. "Hey, my books!"

"You don't want 'em, anyhow!"

He waited for her inside the door. "Your wind's in poor condition, my girl," he taunted. "Better cut out those he-man breakfasts and go in for track."

"Thanks for the advice . . . and carrying the load," she said easily, taking her books from him. The hall was bedlam. She wormed her way toward the bulletin board, ran a practiced eye over old items to find anything of interest that was new.

"Glee Club try-outs this afternoon—3 PM. Room 104. Apply to Miss Haynes. Come one, come all."

If there was one thing she loved to do above another it was to sing. She hummed a bar or two under her breath. "That's for me," she decided, and swung down the corridor. "Hi, Judy! Hi, Sam."

2.

Miss Haynes rapped for attention. She was youngish and pretty, and in her two years at Brookhaven High had built the Glee Club into a spirited and accomplished organization. In spite of her appearance, she was known as something of a martinet where her subject was concerned, and it was considered an honor to be among those she chose for this group.

"I'm glad to see so many of you have come out for the

trials," she said now, letting her eye run over the dozen young people gathered in the small practice room. "The Club needs new voices . . . we lose some each year, of course, and have to replace them . . . but aside from that, I think there's nothing like group singing to bring about a feeling of friendliness and cooperation, of working together to produce something beautiful. I suppose you're all anxious to have your voices tried and get away to your dates, so we'll run through the applicants alphabetically, that way we won't seem to play favorites. Any A's—B's—C's?"

Susan sat in the back of the room, resigned to wait. Being a T she would be well down toward the last. But she didn't mind. It would be fun to hear the others and get a line on their ability and also just how Miss Haynes operated.

She was businesslike and quick, but thorough. She had each boy and girl run a few scales, hold high, medium and low notes for breath control, sing a cappella and, if possible, solfeggio, and then do some sight reading.

"Oh dear," she said, after a while, "we seem to be getting mostly sopranos and tenors! And we do need strengthening in the other departments." But she went on . . . and one after the other was dismissed with a word or two of thanks and a promise to let them know if other vacancies occurred.

There were only three of them left now, Susan noticed; herself, a boy whom she had seen around but couldn't place, and a tall, nice-looking Negro girl. Susan looked at her with perfunctory interest—she seemed familiar, but she was in none of her classes; yet she must be a junior or senior. Her hair was sleek and simply drawn to a bun on her neck, her eyes were liquid and alive in her long face, and she had a wide, flexible mouth.

"Next!"

Susan looked around; no one moved. "I suppose I am next," she said, and rose. Miss Haynes wheeled about on her stool.

"Aren't you new?"

"This is my first year at High."

"A freshman?"

"No, a junior," Susan smiled. "I'm just short!"

"What's your name?"

"Susan Trowbridge."

"Oh yes," Miss Haynes said. "I've heard of you."

She said it pleasantly, and Susan thought, It's nice to be recognized after such a short time at the school.

"Well, let's get on . . . another soprano, I suppose."

"I'm afraid so."

"It's nothing to be sorry for . . . except from my angle. We just have a plethora of them this year. However, if you're good I can use you."

After she'd tried her briefly she said, in some surprise, "You *are* good. Have you had training?"

"No," said Susan. "I just like to sing. I sing a great deal —for myself. And the family doesn't seem to mind."

"I shouldn't think they would! You have a good, true voice; nothing powerful, but that's not what I need. It has a sweet tone, and good carrying quality, I'd say. . . . Let's have some sight now, if you will. Here, take this, and see how you read it."

She handed Susan "Marsk Stig's Daughter," a Danish folk song and unfamiliar, even as to title. Susan gave it a hasty run-through; it didn't look too difficult. Miss Haynes banged out the introduction with a kind of weary precision and Susan, sensing something of her tiredness, knew her first nervousness of the afternoon. But she gathered courage as she went along and it seemed to her that Miss Haynes' accompaniment grew better, too. They ended together in a burst of music, and Susan felt flushed and excited.

"Very nice! Very nice indeed. You'll do, my dear, and thanks for coming out. I hope you won't force that sweet voice of yours; it will grow and be something you can be proud of. You can train for strength, but never for quality." She looked around.

"Now where has that boy gone?"

The Negro girl spoke up. "He left, Miss Haynes, just a few minutes ago."

Miss Haynes gave a brief smile. "Stage fright, probably . . . or too many girls to suit him." Just the same she was annoyed, one could see. "I do need more boys' voices. . . . Oh well, he would possibly have turned out to be another tenor. You're next, then, and last." She gave a shake to her shoulders. "You must be way down in the alphabet?"

"I'm Beth Varley," the Negro girl said and rose swiftly to come up to the piano.

"Ummm. Soprano too?"

"No, Miss Haynes. I sing contralto."

Miss Haynes looked up with quick interest. "I thought I'd never get one. Let's hear you."

Susan tiptoed to the back of the room again. She was curious to hear this girl's voice. And besides, it would only take a few minutes more.

Miss Haynes ran a preliminary scale. "Sing that," she said, and Beth Varley opened her mouth and sang.

Susan sat bolt upright. A tingle ran along her spine. The voice was as smooth as cream, rich and full. You could almost see a column as she sang. And it had an electric quality, as if something vital and fresh had swept through the room, filling it.

The Glee Club director sat still for a moment. Susan wondered if she was feeling the same shock of pleasure that *she* had experienced. It seemed almost, when the silence prolonged itself, as if she were making up her mind about something.

After another moment she flipped through the music on the rack, and jerked out a folder. "With a voice like that, it hardly matters whether you can do sight reading or not, I suppose," she said in her brusque fashion. "But try it anyhow."

It was "Ave Maria," by Bach-Gounod, and difficult. But Beth sang it with ease and feeling, her hands folded loosely in front of her. She looked happy when she sang, and Susan felt the same happiness permeating her own mind.

Miss Haynes gathered up the sheets, stacked them neatly, closed the piano. "I can certainly use a contralto voice like that. You'll probably carry the whole section . . . though my aim is to get a blending, not just a few fine voices. I have to run along now. Thank you both. It was really a very profitable afternoon. Next rehearsal is Thursday, directly after school. You'll be there?"

"Yes, Miss Haynes," they echoed. The director gave a quick look around the room to see that everything was left in order and herded them in front of her. In the corridor she gave them a bright nod and hurried off in one direction, while Beth and Sue took the other in leisurely fashion.

Sue felt excited. She hummed a few bars from the melody Beth had just sung. "Your voice is absolutely thrilling!" she said warmly. "I got goose pimples all over . . . I love that sensation."

Beth smiled. Her eyes shone. "You're nice to say that. It's what music ought to do to people."

"Yes, but it depends on the way a person puts it over . . . I don't know, either. Maybe it's mostly the voice. I had tingles down my spine when you just sang the scale."

Beth laughed now. It was a good sound, full and throaty. It was more like the quality of her singing, with the same warmth and depth. When she spoke her voice was higher and softer than you'd imagine, knowing she was a contralto.

"Of course you've studied singing?" Sue asked conversationally.

"Some. Not as much as I'd like."

Maybe I shouldn't have asked, Sue thought swiftly. She knew nothing about Beth Varley. Maybe singing lessons were out of the question for her. She said quickly, "You hardly need them anyhow. Your voice is so true and easy. You ought to do something with it."

"I want to," Beth answered. They passed out of the big main doors together and sauntered down the walk. "I want to be a singer."

"That's wonderful! You *should* be."

"Yes. Only it takes money. And such a long training. Sometimes I think I shouldn't even dream of it . . . and then again, it seems that it's the only thing in the world I *must* do."

"I wish I felt that way about something," Sue said, a little wistfully.

"Perhaps you have a lot of things to choose from," Beth said. "Your own voice is lovely; you could do radio work—"

"Oh, it's nothing special and I know it. And even if it were, I don't know that I'd want to study singing. You have to have such—such devotion, and discipline, and even so, it's a hard life, they say."

"I know that," Beth replied with a serious air. "I've never fooled myself about how hard it is. In fact, I don't think anyone—like myself—could come even this far without realizing it." They walked on together companionably. "But," Beth continued, "I wouldn't mind how hard it was if I could get somewhere . . . if I could do the thing I want to do."

"You will," Sue assured her. "Why not? I guess all—artists have a hard time."

Beth nodded. "And some more than others," she said quietly.

Sue thought she knew what Beth meant, but she didn't quite know what to say that wouldn't sound—well, awkward. "Do any of the rest of your family sing?" she asked instead.

Beth's face broke into a smile, as if just thinking about

her family was pleasant. "Oh, my, yes! Mother's always singing; Dad used to be in a church choir, and my sister —the one who's a teacher in the South—sang a lot when she was home. But she never wanted to *be* a singer, the way I do."

"Have you lived here long?" Sue asked. "I seem to be asking an awful number of questions," she apologized, "but you see, we're new here."

"I was born in Brookhaven," Beth explained. "So were all my brothers and sisters—but Mother came from Georgia and Dad from South Carolina. Dad's a doctor, you know."

No, Sue thought, she didn't know. Doctor Varley. She'd never heard of him. "Of medicine?" she said, hesitantly.

"An M. D., yes. He's a general practitioner . . . they seem to be most needed, Dad says, and he's always busy."

Sue ran over in her mind the doctors she had heard mentioned. Dr. Randall—and Dr. Severance—and Pitkin —and Mulholland . . . and their own Doctor Marsh. . . . "Is he on the hospital staff?"

Beth said calmly, "He's never been admitted to the hospital staff, though he's practiced here twenty years."

Sue wanted to say, "That's odd!" and thought better of it. It was queer how, in just this short time, she had run up against several blind alleys. Maybe when she knew Beth better—

"You said 'all your brothers and sisters,' " she reminded Beth now. "Tell me about them."

"Well," Beth said promptly, "there's Lulu—that's short for Lulu-Belle, named for my grandmother. She's the eldest and the one who's a teacher at Frogmore, down South. She always wanted to teach and she loves it. And my older brother Hank is in the Army. He's in Europe—we heard from him again just yesterday. And my other sister, Marge, is working part-time and studying nights to be a laboratory technician."

"That *is* interesting," Sue said with warmth.

"And then there's Chuckles . . . we call him that; his real name's Stuart. Chuckles is eight; he's the baby of the family, and as cute as a button." Her voice was colored with her affection. "A little scamp most of the time, and spoiled, I'm afraid, but cute! And he *can* be as good as gold."

Sue laughed. "I have one like that, too—only he's nine. Kenny. I know just what you mean."

"They do liven up the place, don't they?" Beth commented. "Chuckles is always thinking up some devilment . . . but he's not bad, you know; just full of mischief. *He* wants to be a fireman right now."

"Kenny's gone in for airplane piloting! If he makes another model plane I'll go crazy—they're so noisy. He knows one jet from another, though, which is more than I do."

They talked on animatedly, comparing brothers. Sue shifted her books from one arm to another. They were passing Schmidt's. "Look, I'm parched! Let's wet our whistles . . . between chalk dust and that singing I could do with something cold."

"Oh, I'm due home this minute," Beth said. "Here's where I turn off anyway. Mother said she wanted to get out for an errand and I'll have to round up Chuckles and start supper."

Sue was disappointed. "Well, I don't want one by myself." Perhaps she should have indicated that it was her treat. But she couldn't very well, without looking in her change purse and counting up. As it was, she doubted if she had more than twenty cents left, after buying that ball pen and her lunch and paying her A. C. dues . . . it was probably a good thing that Beth *couldn't* come along.

"Okay, then," she said. "I'll be seeing you again."

"At Glee Club," Beth answered. "It was nice talking to you."

She turned, with a salute of her hand, and walked down Main. Her black hair shone in the light, her back was straight, she carried her head well. Miss Phillips, of Physical Ed., would approve. Sue thought, I could do with a little posture improvement myself. Glory, but she was thirsty! She'd have to hurry home and save money.

The front door was open and she thought she heard voices and saw shadowed movements behind the living-room curtains. As she mounted the porch steps her mother came to the screen and flung it open. "Where have you *been*?" she cried excitedly. "I thought you'd never get home! Carol's here, and she's brought the baby. Tim left them right after lunch, and he'll pick them up Friday when he comes back from Scranton with the car. Isn't that wonderful?"

3.

Sue threw her books on the hall table and ran in to grab Carol in a bear hug.

"Hey, my ribs!" Carol groaned.

"Would you rather it was your neck?" Sue grinned. "You're my favorite sister; I have to let you know it."

"That's nice—and me the only one you have."

"Well, think how terrible it would be if you were my only sister and *weren't* my favorite! . . . Where's Precious Lamb?"

"Upstairs finishing her nap. I thought she could have a little longer one than usual because it was quite a tiring trip."

"Why in the world didn't you let us know you were coming? I'd have done up your room and killed the fatted calf and knitted Her Majesty a new sweater."

"It was awfully sudden. We did call Mom this morning and she said to come right along, it would be a grand surprise for you and Kenny."

Kenny, as if hearing his name, stuck his head around the door. "Sis, does she sleep all day? She'll be dopey."

His mother cast a practiced eye over him. "I see you've been having a snack. Wipe the butter off your chin, Kenny."

He ran a quick hand across his chin. "Gosh, if she doesn't wake up soon I'm going out with Fred. I've been waiting all afternoon."

Mrs. Trowbridge laughed. "Forty-one minutes, to be exact. You might go up and see if she's awake, Kenny." He tore up the stairs and she called after him, "But don't pick her up! Call me."

Sue took her sister by the shoulders and wheeled her around. "You look wonderful. Doesn't she, Mom? Married life agrees with her."

"Why wouldn't it . . . when it's with Tim?" Carol said with a happy smile.

"Don't sound so smug, young lady," her mother said affectionately. "But I'm glad you feel that way."

Susan pulled her sister down on the couch. "Come on, tell me all about it."

"All about being a married lady in ten minutes? No can do . . . I'm still learning."

"It takes a lifetime," Mrs. Trowbridge said.

Kenny's voice, full of excitement, came bellowing down the stairwell. "Mom, Mom, she's stuck her whole fist in her mouth! Maybe she's hungry!"

Carol chuckled. "I hope he doesn't try to feed her gumdrops. He's feeling very important since I called him Uncle Kenny."

Sue grinned. "I know how he feels. I can hardly get over being Aunt Sue myself . . . and it's awfully funny to think of Kenny as an uncle. Perhaps it will tone him down, if he thinks he has to act the part."

It was fun having Carol in the house again. She was six years older, but they had always been very close, and it had been a tremendous wrench when Carol married and moved away. At first she thought she would never get used to it—it was, as she told her friends, as if part of her had been amputated. Carol was no letter-writer, and so it was harder than it might have been to have her go away, but even her sketchy notes had given the unmistakable impression that she was happy and enjoying her nomadic life. For she had followed Tim to camp and from one camp to another, living in small furnished apartments, one time in just a single room, and meeting other young women from all over the country. Tim had been in Viet Nam only four months when he was invalided home, and Carol lived in Baltimore while he was hospitalized there. When he was well again they had taken a tiny house in Connecticut where he had a job as expediter for a machinery concern . . . and this was her first visit home since that important move.

There was so much to talk about that Mr. Trowbridge came home before they had even started dinner. His face broke into a broad smile when he saw his other daughter and his grandchild, and he was full of questions. "I'm glad this happened before I had to leave on that trip—"

"Oh, Henry, another one?" his wife asked.

"Well, the one I told you about; only it's come up a little sooner than I expected. I'll leave tomorrow early and be back in a couple of weeks, if all goes well."

"I *was* hoping you'd be here for that social at the church," Mrs. Trowbridge said, a little wistfully. "It's such a nice chance to get acquainted. And I wouldn't want to go alone."

"I'll go with you, Mom," Sue said.

"Thank you, dear. But it's not the same thing. . . . Oh well—"

"After all, my love, a salesman's lot is mostly travel."

"Yes, I know." She sighed. "We do want to get to know some of the nice people here in town; this would have been such a good opportunity; the women seemed most pleasant." Then she straightened. "We won't think about it now. Kenny, take your bike and go and get some ice-cream at Schmidt's—"

"I'll walk," Kenny said. "I'll walk fast."

Carol hooted. "I never thought I'd live to hear this! Are you trying to reduce, Kenny?"

"My bike's got a flat," he stated belligerently. "Some kid musta put a nail in the tire at school."

"Why didn't you fix it this afternoon?" Mr. Trowbridge inquired reasonably.

"Well, gosh, Pop, I had to watch the baby!"

"You wanted to, you mean," his mother said. "If you hurry, you can still change your tire and get down to Schmidt's—"

"I'll do it tonight," he offered. "Or in the morning."

"You'll fix it now," his father stated from behind his paper. "And get a move on, Kenny. Nothing ever fixed itself, and nothing ever got done by putting it off." Kenny hesitated a moment and then started toward the door. His father called after him, "If you need some help, whistle. But I guess anybody who makes model planes can wrestle with a little old bicycle tire."

"Oh sure," Kenny said, somewhat restored in his ego. "Wanta watch me?"

His father chuckled. "Tell me about it—afterwards."

When he was safely out of the room Carol laughed. "It sounds just like a familiar record. I could believe I'd never been away!"

Her mother said comically, "Sometimes I wonder if he'll *ever* grow up!"

"Don't worry, Laura," Mr. Trowbridge said equably. "It'll happen overnight, one of these days . . . and as likely as not you'll be sorry when it does."

"If I live till the time comes," Laura Trowbridge groaned. "Well, I must stir myself. Supper will be late as it is."

"Come upstairs while I get Angel-Face ready for bed," Carol said to Sue, "and we can talk."

Sue followed her with alacrity. It was good to have Carol to herself, if only for half an hour. There was so much she wanted to ask, so much she wanted to hear about. As they talked, in the old, free way, the years seemed to disappear and it was like the days before Carol had married.

"Remember that little room we shared in Warren?"

"Do I? And you always spilling over onto my side of the dresser and hogging more than your share of hangers in the closet!"

"I like that! You never bought any padded hangers and always 'borrowed' mine and forgot to give them back and then thought they were yours!"

"As glib a fibber as ever. . . . Well, now you have a room all to yourself. Aren't you happy?"

Sue gave Carol a hug. "I'd rather have you back, spilled powder and everything. If that's an admission of weakness, make the most of it."

"Sweet Sue! You like it here, don't you?"

"Love it. You would, too."

"I'm happy where I am. . . . What about Mother? I can't quite make it out."

"Oh, she does, too."

"But what about those neighbors? They seem to bother her. She talked about them, off and on, at intervals all afternoon."

"They're pretty messy."

"The house does have a ratty appearance. But there's always something. A neighbor of mine used to light a fire in her incinerator whenever I'd hung out the laundry."

Sue made a face. "What did you do?"

"I didn't wash for two weeks and she piled up so much trash she *had* to burn it . . . a whole raft of it. And then I did a big laundry, and when she came out to see it I grinned at her, and she smiled back after a bit and we've been friends ever since."

"Oh, the Garritys are willing to be friendly enough. They practically use this garden like their own. That's one of the things that gripes Mom."

They talked, but it *was* different. It dawned on Sue after a bit. Little phrases—'when I went to Groper's'—'The Findlays were over'—'Tim's Aunt Mary telephoned and sent us over a couple of chairs.' Things she didn't know about. A new life; a new group of friends. A world of her own for Carol.

Sue sensed the change as the hour wore on. It wasn't that Carol meant to be different . . . but how could she help being? She had a husband now, a child, a circle of friends who were strangers to her family. And though she wanted to be interested in what Sue and Kenny and her parents were doing, her main interest was in her own concerns. It was right; it was the way it should be. But it left Sue feeling a little alone, and she shivered once, and wondered why, for she wasn't *cold*. . . .

Take the way Carol dismissed the Garritys, for instance. And the way she asked what Sue had been doing.

"I went to Glee Club try-out," Sue answered. "That's why I was late."

"Did you get in?" Carol said idly, turning little Dena over her knee and working deftly with diaper and pins.

"Oh yes. There was a girl, though, who has the most marvelous voice!" Sue's voice was colored with her remembering. "It's beautiful . . . she'll be heard from one of these days. I walked home with her. She wants to be a singer."

"What's her name?"

"Beth Varley. Her father's a doctor."

"Oh?" Carol wasn't too interested. "Hand me that talc, will you, Sue? . . . I'm glad you're getting on. You would, though. You have the knack of making friends."

"You're prejudiced."

"No, I'm not," Carol managed between the pins. "If you can make a friend of your sister you can manage anybody."

"Thanks for those kind words."

Sue kept an eye out for Beth Varley on her way to school next morning; she was anxious to talk to her again. But she did not see her and, in fact, met no one she knew till she was going up the walk.

Then she spied Judy Riggs. "All set for History exam today?" she greeted her.

Judy looked around, saw who it was, hesitated a moment, and then fell into step beside her. "Is one ever?" she asked drily.

"Not this one. Today less than usual. My sister is visiting us with her baby and distractions are too numerous to mention. I'm afraid I spent the minimum on History last night. Can you give me a capsule of the life of Charles II before we go up the front steps?"

"No, but I can give you a bit of advice."

How funny that sounded, Sue thought. Or was it something in Judy's voice? She must be imagining things. "What's the matter? Does my slip show or is my lipstick on crooked?"

"Neither. You look all right." Sue thought she detected a slight emphasis on the word 'look' but she couldn't be sure.

"What then?"

Instead of answering directly Judy asked another question. "Did you walk home from school yesterday with Beth Varley?"

"Yes," Sue answered at once. "Do you know her?"

"I know who she is," Judy said distinctly.

"She was at Glee Club try-outs with me. We got to talking. Her voice *does* things to you. Did you ever hear her?"

Judy said, "No."

Sue looked at her, but Judy was looking straight ahead. They mounted the steps together; Sue held open the heavy door and Judy stepped through. On the other side she waited for Sue. Her eyes roved over the crowds milling in the hallway. "I've got to run. . . . My advice is, Don't."

"Don't what?" Sue was genuinely puzzled.

"Don't walk with Beth Varley. Or any Negro, for that matter."

"But—" Sue almost sputtered. "Why, it was the most natural thing . . . there we were, in try-outs together, the last ones, as a matter of fact, and then we got to talking and we started out together and kept going till she had to turn off—" Suddenly it struck her that she was making unnecessary explanations. "What is this, anyway? How did you know?"

"Someone saw you."

"Who?"

"Someone," Judy repeated. "That sort of thing gets around. If you want to get along here, you just won't do it, that's all."

"Well, but—" Sue's eyes felt hot.

"I'm only telling you for your own good. It simply isn't done in Brookhaven. And not at Brookhaven High, either."

"It seems to me," Sue said heatedly, "you're taking a lot on yourself, and making a lot out of nothing, for that matter."

"I'm just telling you how it is," Judy said calmly, almost indifferently. "We like you here, and we thought maybe you didn't know. But take it or leave it. It's up to you."

4.

The more she thought about the incident the more up-set Sue became. She tried *not* to think of it, shutting it out of her mind deliberately, but it came creeping back, pervading her thoughts like an unpleasant odor. It ran-kled, somehow. And yet Judy had probably been doing what she thought was the right thing, Sue had to admit to herself. She hadn't sounded angry; just warning. And Sue recalled that Judy *had* said, "We like you here." Well, that was something.

But what am I? Sue argued with her silent self. *Am I somebody who does things—or doesn't do them—just so I can be liked? I'd be a worm that way. No, not a worm —a chameleon. Changing my colors according to the atmosphere around me. Being one thing for one person, another for another.*

"For the second time, Sue, will you demonstrate the fourteenth problem on the board?"

Sue leaped to her feet, knocking her pen on the floor. Ben Travis stooped to retrieve it. "Oh, where are my wandering thoughts tonight?" he warbled, *sotto voce.*

"No prompting, Ben," Miss Thwaite's voice cut in.

"I'm sorry, Miss Thwaite," Sue said. "I was—I was—"

"Wool-gathering," Miss Thwaite said pleasantly enough. "You can make up for it by giving us a superior demonstration."

Sue drew up the problem, but when she began on "Let ABC equal CDE" and "Angle DEF equals—" she got tangled and couldn't recall just what she had said. The problem bogged down into a hopeless mess of letters and Miss Thwaite said finally, "It *is* a demonstration—of a sort. But not the sort I wanted. . . . Judy—"

Judy tripped to the board and whizzed through the statement to the solution. When she passed Sue on her way back to her desk she gave her a pleasant smile.

I'm silly to keep thinking about it, Sue decided. *But it had come so unexpectedly, and the whole idea was so silly. . . . Just because I walked down the street with Beth and talked to her. . . .* She was beginning to feel warm again, warm with annoyance.

She looked around the room with new interest. There were no Negroes in this class. There *were* Negroes in some of her other classes. She hadn't noticed them particularly before, but she had been aware of them at first because at Warren there had been only three or four in the entire High School, and none in any of her classes.

Brookhaven was different altogether. It had a fairly large Negro population; you saw Negroes in the shops and on the streets in good numbers. Did they live a life apart—in the city but not of it? She knew nothing about them, really. Just as Doctor Varley's name had been unknown to her; yet he must be known among his own people.

Was Judy's attitude the attitude of Brookhaven itself, or just Judy's own? She'd have to find out, if only to settle the gnawing little annoyance in her mind. But even so, Judy's attitude didn't have to be hers . . . *wasn't* hers. Did you have to conform to what the Judys wanted? Couldn't you act on your own—even here at school? Particularly here at school?

I'm making a mountain out of a molehill, she shook herself angrily. Forget it. Judy has forgotten it. Just the way she smiled at you on her way to her seat showed that. Maybe she was having a fit of pique when she spoke. Maybe it was just a quirk of hers that you have to ignore. There are people like that . . . people with a blind spot. Forget it. What I am going to have for lunch is the important question right now.

David Grinnell sought her out in the cafeteria. "Don't eat too much!" he shouted above the din. "I'm treating to cokes this afternoon and I want you to appreciate 'em."

"I have to fortify myself for the session," she shot back.

He grinned back, expertly lifting his tray above the heads of half a dozen girls and worming his way toward a table. "You'll eat those words—if nothing else!"

Sue slid into a place between Dorr Kittredge and Gracie Bowman. While they chattered she let her gaze travel over the room. There were three long tables of Negroes eating together. Because they wanted to? Possibly they preferred it that way. No doubt they had things to talk over just as her own group did. It was queer how she had never noticed this before. Yet they must always have been there, together. They were talking and laughing, a couple of the boys shoving each other good-naturedly. She looked sharply for Beth, but did not see her. But that meant nothing. She may have missed classes today. Or perhaps she could go home to lunch. Or brought her own and ate it upstairs, the way some of them did.

"Your conversation slays me!" Dorr said extravagantly. "You could understudy a deaf and dumb woman any day."

"I'm sorry," Sue said, pulling herself back to her companions.

"You'd better be," Gracie said affably. "Dorr has asked you three times if the coffee jelly's any good . . . or are you refusing to answer because it might incriminate you?"

"What long words you use, Gracie," Dorr teased. "Don't you know that romantic far-away look when you see it? You used to have it yourself last year over Boyd Allen."

"I don't even remember him," Gracie said, digging into

her banana roll. "And I'm sure I never looked like *that*. Is he worth it—whoever he is?"

" 'Whoever he is,' " Dorr scoffed. "If you had eyes in your head you'd know it was David Grinnell. . . . Look, she's so far gone she doesn't even hear me!"

"I hear you all right," Sue retorted. "You're just being silly."

"No, I'm not. I'm not blaming you, either. He's nice, but nice. Only—let me warn you, my girl—you've got competition. Half the gals in High think the same, and the other half just haven't good sense."

Sue laughed. "Which half do you belong to?"

Gracie hooted. "She's got you there, Dorr! Serves you right for sticking your neck out."

Sue was glad in a way that their attention had been diverted from her preoccupation, even if it took this form of ribbing. And she was glad, too, that they had not been aware of the real reason for her preoccupation. For how could she explain it?

"David's a good kid," Dorr said, suddenly a little serious. "Mixed up in everything, but not stuffy about it. You're in luck that he's your co."

"I still don't get how I happened to be paired with him on this committee," Sue said frankly.

Gracie answered her with equal frankness. She had a pert nose and laughing blue eyes, and her candid expression took any sting from the words. "Well, you know, don't you, that Helen Olds was slated for the job, but her parents decided to send her to Junior College this year, and that left a hole. Nobody else specially wanted the job because they all knew how much work it would be. Helen was the kind—like David—that didn't mind. So . . ." she drew out the word comically, "you were new here and you looked sort of cute, and willing, and—well, ignorant about the set-up—so we picked you!"

"More truth than poetry, anyhow," Sue said equably. "I knew there was a reason, but I didn't know it was quite so unflattering. In other words, you picked me for a sucker?"

"Gracie didn't mean that," Dorr said, on an anxious note. "You do put things crudely, Gracie. Of course," she turned to Sue, "anybody in his right mind would know that you got the job for a couple of reasons that weren't on the surface. After all, you *were* new, and we didn't know too much about you . . . but, well, it's a compliment in a way, because, even if we tagged you with a job none of us wanted much, we thought you looked like the kind who could pull it off."

Sue clapped her hands over her ears. "Don't tell me any more or I'll be a pricked balloon! You two can certainly deflate a person."

Dorr leaned over and patted her shoulder. "Gosh, Sue, we didn't mean to be brutal. You asked for it—I mean, you wanted to know why—"

"And now I do," Sue said swiftly. "Leave it at that. Fact is, I don't really mind the work—"

"And, brother, there's going to be plenty!"

Sue nodded. "And I rather like the idea of proving myself early in the game."

"That's what we thought," Gracie said, spooning up

the last of her sauce. "See? A compliment to you . . . and we don't have to work!"

"What are you planning?" Dorr asked.

"I'm seeing Dave this afternoon," Sue answered. "We're to hash it out then. Any ideas you want put over?"

"Of course not! Why do you think we shoved all this off on you? Just make it good."

"And different," Gracie interjected. "Everybody's tired of the same old colored streamers and Bob Gray's Orchestra and lemon pop."

"But don't forget the expenses."

"We need to make money rather than spend it."

"And give us a chance to get new formals."

"The boys don't like it."

"Who cares?"

"But if they won't come, why have a dance?"

The bell rang and Sue leaped up. "Thank heavens! You've got me utterly confused by now."

"Just what we intended!" they both said together. "See you tomorrow."

David Grinnell met her outside the doors at three o'clock. "Prompt!" he said approvingly. "One in a million, I guess, so I won't get my hopes up."

"I was anxious to get it over with," Sue twitted him.

"We're only beginning. You'll have a long time to bear up."

"I can stand it if you can."

"Any ideas?"

"A lot of negative ones. That is, some of the girls were telling me what they *don't* want."

"You always get that."

"Yes, and out of it sometimes comes a real brainstorm. I think I feel one blowing up this minute, as a matter of fact."

"Let's get to cover then!" he laughed, putting a hand under her elbow and hurrying her along.

David was a popular boy and was continually being hailed, Sue noticed, by passing groups. "Hi, Dave!" "Out on parole, boy?" "What—using your feet today?"

Many of the couples were sauntering, she knew, towards Schmidt's. When they got there and found a booth she looked around. There were a good many she recognized, quite a few whom she knew to speak to . . . everybody laughing, joking over orders, talking over the day's adventures. With sharpened interest Sue observed that there were no Negroes present . . . just as she recalled, now, that she had not seen any mixed couples on the street. No wonder she had been conspicuous. She wondered, though, why there were no Negroes here, and spoke of it—she hoped casually—to Dave.

"Oh, this is our hang-out," he said easily.

She picked that up. "Ours?" she said. "What do you mean?"

"Well, what I say. Yours, mine—" he gestured—"theirs."

"There's no law against the others coming here, is there?"

"Of course not. It's just a sort of—mutual understanding, I guess. What are you going to have?"

No wonder Beth had not wanted to come in with her!

I hope I didn't embarrass her, Sue thought. I wouldn't have suggested it, if I'd known.

David was saying, "A triple-threat?"

"Cokes is what you suggested."

"Yes, but I'm feeling expansive. Expansive, not expensive. How about a double-decker then?"

"No, just an orange ice."

"Girls and their figures!" he snorted. "Can you think on that?"

"Wait and see."

"I'll order some peanut butter crackers then. Proteins." When their orders came he said, "Now, out with the brainstorm."

"Well," Sue let some of the orange ice melt and trickle in delicious coolness down her throat, "you hear on every hand that it has to be different, and not cost too much, and not mean too much work."

"You got the idea."

"And at the same time everybody tells you what marvels the Seniors worked a couple of years ago with that Evening in Paris stunt, with the auditorium decked out with restaurant fronts and a little park and statuary and a fountain and stars set in the ceiling—"

David groaned. "They'll never forget it. But that was sheer inspiration. What's more, they were out to impress themselves. We're only Juniors and all we've got to impress are the Frosh."

Sue nodded. "Fortunately. At the same time nobody wants the same old thing, as they put it, and yet they want it to look gay and they want to dance."

"That's the ticket. What's the answer?"

"I thought," Sue said slowly, "that it would be fun to have a barn dance."

"Boy! The auditorium's a barn, all right!"

"Exactly. It wouldn't take much to transform it, either. Corn shocks and pumpkins, some piles of hay, lanterns—"

"Wooden tables for refreshments—"

"Everybody in dungarees and dirndls—"

"*Boys* in dungarees, *girls* in dirndls," David said emphatically, and Sue laughed.

"Of course! Whoever saw a boy in a dirndl?"

"Trouble is," he said darkly, "there are too many girls in dungarees."

"That's why this will be different. We could have square dances to set everybody off. A hillbilly orchestra, and a caller."

"Where do we get 'em?"

"That's up to you. You know this town and environs better than I do."

"Okay," he took on the job easily. "I'll settle for that end of it, since you've dreamed up the idea. I think we can sell it to our committee, particularly if we choose the right ones to be *on* the committee."

"I'll count on you to suggest names, then. I don't know enough people . . . yet."

"Right." He looked at her, his eyes bright with interest. "I think we'll get on, you and I. You and me. You and I."

"Anyhow, the two of us!" she grinned back at him. "By the way, we ought to have some of the Negro students on some of the committees." She said it lightly, and waited

... she was scarcely aware of how breathlessly she waited.

"Well, I guess so. Sure. Make 'em work, too. Tickets, maybe, and decorations."

Words rose to her lips, but she bit them down. He had done this much. He had fallen in with her suggestion, even though his way of phrasing it had been a little unfortunate, she thought. But she brushed that aside. She liked David. She was glad he liked her. She was especially glad that he had given his approval to her 'brainstorm.' That meant that it would go through, and they would be working together for weeks to come. It was a pleasant prospect, and she was happy over it.

"Fall to," he ordered. "And finish those crackers. Brains like yours have to be nourished. I've got to take good care that you don't flop by the wayside and leave me with the whole shebang to look after!"

5.

Tim came for his wife and baby on Friday, and suddenly they were gone again, in a flurry of last-minute messages and hugs and promises to 'do it soon again.'

Sue felt lost. It made her realize how much she missed Carol to have had just this glimpse of her. But Carol, though she had been happy to be in the bosom of her family once more, was even happier to go with Tim. That, Sue supposed, was what marriage did to you.

"And so it should," her mother said, though she, too, had a somewhat woebegone look.

Kenny was disconsolate. "I miss her already," he said, stuffing his hands in his pockets and turning his head aside. They knew he meant Dena, and not Carol. "It's nice having a baby in the house. You can talk to her, and she doesn't talk back."

"That blissful state of affairs wouldn't last long," Sue said.

Kenny looked hopefully at his mother. "I wouldn't mind having a baby sister, Mom."

She laughed. "You wouldn't mind having one, but would you *mind* one?" She put her hands on his shoulders and gave him a little shove. "Run along now, and clear up the yard."

"Again?"

"Again."

The house seemed preternaturally quiet when Sue came home, but it wore off somewhat as she grew busier and busier at school. David had set things in motion almost at once, and committees were shaping up. True to his promise he had asked George Bellowes to serve on the tickets and Fern Hodges on decorations. Both had accepted with quiet pleasure, and Sue, meeting them, had felt they would do a good job. The idea of a barn dance had met with surprising enthusiasm, and David came to her one day mopping his brow.

"The worst is over. I've found a caller."

"I knew you would."

"Well, *I* didn't. They don't grow on every forsythia

bush. Matter of fact, I had to turn detective to locate one. A boy who works at Joe's Garage heard a customer telling about a country dance they had at Milltown and I asked him who the customer was, but he didn't know."

"So what did you do?"

"I wrote to the Trenton License Bureau for his name . . . the garage man remembered his license! And then I went to see the man, but he was out of town that day."

Sue giggled. "You didn't give up, I know. You—"

"I," he took her up, "asked his wife instead. She gave me the name of the caller they'd had, but when I located him he said it was too far ahead—he might have rheumatism by then!"

"Oh, David!"

"I'm glad you sympathize with me after the job you wished on me."

"You offered to take it."

"Under your influence," he retorted. "However, this rheumatic chap had a friend who might do . . . and I went to see *him*—he lived fifteen miles from there. As luck would have it he didn't have arthritis or other dates, so I signed him up. You can see how I spent last Saturday."

"Out of mischief, anyhow."

"And I saw a lot of the countryside," he said drolly.

"Is he any good?"

"You want that, *too*?" he cried.

"Well, but is he?"

"He said he'd been doing it 'nigh onto forty years,' so I

figured he must know a thing or two. Anyhow, all we can do now is wait and see!"

The committees functioned with a will. This was going to be the best Junior-Freshman Hop ever. Groups of boys brought home jalopies full of corn and pumpkins. Girls fashioned paper lanterns to hang from the beams. They decided to drape the walls with yellow and brown paper, ceiling to floor; some from the art department would paint country scenes which were to be pasted over the windows, so that the effect was as if you were looking out from the barn across rolling fields to brooks and hills. Piles of hay, brought in piecemeal, would serve as seats around the hall; trestle tables were to be laid with checked cloths and pottery bowls of flowers and laden with refreshments. The tickets were all sold; the boys invested in new plaid shirts and gay kerchiefs; the girls were busy pressing their full skirts and sewing on bright blouses.

"They've done a wonderful job," Sue said gratefully.

"Swell. Not a thing missing, except the orchestra and caller."

"We ought to give the committee a party, don't you think?"

"No, I don't. Do you?"

Sue laughed. "Yes, I do. Show them how much we appreciate them."

"Won't words do?"

"Deeds speak louder than words," she reminded him. "We could throw a coke party at—" Then she paused. "Well, some place."

He groaned. "Schmidt's, of course. You *would* think of something like a party."

"And invite everybody," she went on.

"Well—"

"Everybody on the committee has done a real piece of work. We couldn't have some and not the others."

He seemed about to say something, looked at her quizzically. "Go ahead and invite 'em, then. And what do we do for money, if I may be so bold as to ask?"

"We divide the cost," Sue told him, laughing. "It's part of the penalty of being chairmen. You can work an extra hour and I can baby-sit for two."

"Gratitude comes high," he said. "Let me know how many are coming."

Sue asked them at once; there were only three days left before the Hop and she set the time for after school of the day preceding the dance. "That way," she said to each one, "we can check on last-minute items and have a good time in the bargain."

They foregathered in high spirits; Schmidt's was bedlam with the milling group. Sue looked them over.

"Everybody's here but George and Fern."

"Oh, they won't come," someone said.

"But I asked them, and they said they could."

"Maybe so. But they won't come, take my word for it."

"Are you *sure* they said they'd come?" David asked.

She thought back. "George said he would if his father didn't need him."

David nodded. "So his father needed him."

"And Fern," Sue said more slowly, "thought she could

make it unless her mother went to New York and then she'd have to stay home."

"So her mother went to New York and she had to stay home."

Sue looked at him in surprise. His meaning was unmistakably clear; his tone of voice made it doubly so. The others were watching her curiously. She bit her lip. She would not express herself here. Besides, she hardly knew *what* to say. She had, in a way, brought this on herself. She remembered how David had looked at her with that quizzical expression. He had meant that she would find out that some of them would *not* come, and he had been right. But though he had been right, the situation wasn't. It was unfair, and no one seemed to mind but herself.

"We might as well go on, then," she said, trying to make her voice light. "Let's all sit at the two big tables in the rear, and everybody order what he likes."

"Sky the limit?" they teased her.

"So long as it doesn't come to more than a tall coke," she told them.

The party was a success, Sue decided, if you could judge by the noise and the laughter. But for her there was an underlying note of dissatisfaction. The party—in her own mind, at least—had been meant for everyone. It was wrong that two of the group who had worked so hard should have had to miss the fun. And it wasn't that they were ill or prevented from coming. It was that they felt they weren't wanted, and it must have been a strong feeling to keep them away.

When the party broke up David said, "See you tomorrow. I have to stop at Larkin's for Dad's shoes."

"Everything's under control," she said. "I hope it goes off as well as it promises to."

"It will," he assured her. "Just don't break a leg."

"I expect to do that at the Hop. . . . Oh, by the way, what about speeches?"

"Speeches?" he echoed in horror. "Why bring that up?"

"Isn't the Class President going to 'say a few words'?"

"Yes, I don't see that it's necessary, but he's going to. It's a kind of tradition; the Juniors giving the Frosh some good advice they won't take anyhow. I hope he keeps it short."

"Well, and after that, I thought maybe you—"

"I," he said firmly, "am keeping my mouth shut. As of eight-thirty tomorrow night my job is done. I'm just going to enjoy myself."

"But"—she hesitated—"you know, just a little thank-you speech."

"What were we doing today but thanking them? To the tune of four dollars and sixty-five cents. They don't expect any more—and moreover they're not going to get it. From me."

She said slowly, "*I'd* like to then, Dave. Would you— that is, after the President is through, maybe you could just introduce me. I'd like to tell them publicly how much I appreciate what they did. And the Frosh ought to hear it. I'd keep it very brief."

He said nothing for a long moment. There was that quizzical look again. "Okay," he said finally, "it's your funeral."

The auditorium was really transformed. In the soft light of the dimmed lamps the colors were muted and warm. The lanterns swayed with the currents of air, throwing moving shadows on the waxed floor. Against the drawn curtains of the stage, decorated with huge cut-outs of autumnal scenes, sat the members of the three-piece orchestra, two young men with fiddles and an elderly, bent man with a lined, humorous face, a shock of white hair, and a banjo-mandolin as big as his lap.

Sue felt a surge of pride as she surveyed the scene. It might not be like any barn in existence, but there was an illusion of a barn's interior, and it appeared festive and casual and gay. They had worked like Trojans, all of them, at the last-minute; girls were still bringing in the pottery pitchers of cider, the plates of doughnuts and sandwiches.

Sue watched the couples streaming through the big double doors. Gil Rowe and Sam were taking tickets.

"It *looks* good, anyhow," Sam Hogan told her. "I'll give you a whirl later."

"I'm dead on my feet before it begins," Sue said, "but I'll get over it once they strike up."

"You'd better," he warned. "It's bad enough managing my own feet without toting any limp carcasses around."

Even Miss Reynolds and Mr. Hatch, the chaperones,

were in country costume. "It's amazing what all of you have done," Miss Reynolds said, adjusting her neckerchief. "Simply amazing. I'd hardly recognize the place."

"Thank you," Sue said. "That was our aim. Have a good time!"

Drew Millikin, the President, mounted a corner bench; the orchestra stopped thrumming.

"Girls and boys!" he shouted, above the general uproar. They quieted somewhat. "Welcome! You freshmen are practically strangers to us—our paths seldom cross, which is probably a good thing—and some of you look to us seasoned scholars as if you shouldn't be out on a cold night—but welcome, welcome! This Junior-Freshman Hop started away back in antiquity somehow. . . . I did a little research and discovered that it was a dull year along about 1910 and somebody thought to liven things up by having a party. But a party for whom, or what? Both questions seemed to be answered when someone else suggested a party for the Frosh. And it's been going on ever since. We got stung, too. But we're bearing up. We hope you'll take this all in so you can do your stuff when your time comes, which is in two years, and we hope you'll gather from us how to act. Make the most of this night, because tomorrow you'll be back in your lowly places, beneath our notice, and next year we'll be Seniors, so that, even though you'll be Sophs, you won't have much chance to talk to us. But tonight you're our guests; what's more, you're our equals. It only happens once a year and that, so far as I'm concerned, is enough. Let joy be unconfined!"

They laughed and hooted and cheered, glad that it had been short if not sweet. Then David mounted the bench, and they groaned. "What? More yakkety-yak?"

"Cheer up," he said. "It's not *my* idea to add to the general depression by making a speech. I'm only going to say one sentence, and that is: Here is Susan Trowbridge, my co-chairman, who wants to say a few words."

The groans this time were ostentatiously louder. Sue felt her heart thumping painfully. David had promised to introduce her, and so he had. But it was as bad as going in cold. She sensed their impatience and David's not too subtle way of indicating that he had nothing to do with the idea. But she stuck out her chin and mounted the bench.

"I'm going to be almost as brief," she said, raising her voice to ride above the noise of movement. "I just couldn't let this chance go by, because I wanted all of you to know —you Juniors who weren't working on the dance, and you Frosh who are going to have such a good time at it—that David and I appreciate all the terrific work the committees put into this job. Perhaps I appreciate it even more because I'm new here and I had no idea what grand workers you are. That's why I want to thank publicly all of you who helped make this a success. David and I tried to show our gratitude by a little party we gave yesterday, and because George Bellowes who worked on tickets—I heard that he got a friend to print them gratis when the printer's shop was going to charge too much—and Fern Hodges, who is responsible for some of these marvelous decorations—because they couldn't be at the party, here are my thanks now. And applause!" She clapped her hands together hard above her head, and a few hardy souls followed suit.

But she knew at once that it hadn't gone over well. The milling groups set up a buzzing. David raised his hand and the orchestra began to play, a lively tune that called to them. They were talking about this innovation of hers. They hadn't liked it. She cast her eyes hurriedly over the throng before she jumped down, to find George Bellowes and Fern Hodges. To her surprise, they looked unsmiling and somewhat embarrassed. Was Beth Varley here? Yes, there she was, in a group of Negroes. Beth seemed to be gazing in her direction, but it was hard to tell from her masklike face just what she thought. No one seemed pleased, not even the Negro groups. What had she expected, she asked of herself crossly—that they would rush up and thank *her* for thanking *them*?

There was an almost audible shrugging of shoulders. The caller stood up and began to bellow in a voice surprisingly loud for his slight form:

"Hurry, folks, fill the hall.
  Get your partners, one and all. . . .
  With a couple here and a couple there,
  We'll start the dance when you form your square."

He cajoled the reluctant ones from the side-lines, he got the squares formed with even numbers of couples, and he started them through their first steps, all in verse. His voice filled every corner of the auditorium, there was no escaping him, nor his eagle eye, either.

> "Now spread out wide—room for all—
> Square your sets and wait for the call."

When he had them to his satisfaction he shouted, "Honor your partners!" and the evening really began.

There was not a dull moment after that. He taught them the patterns of the dances, patiently and with humor, and the hall was like a kaleidoscope of color and movement, the gay skirts of the girls and the bright shirts of the boys weaving in and out, forming and re-forming to his shouted instructions and his sing-song voice.

> "First couple right and circle four. . . ."
> "The bird in the cage and close the door. . . ."
> "The bird step out and the crow hop in. . . ."
> "Then those two couples take a swing. . . ."

There were mistakes and laughter; those with a natural rhythm and a quick ear managed to steer the others, dazed but willing, into the proper formations.

Sue, swinging from one outstretched hand to another, do-si-do-ing her partner, who was do-si-do-ing likewise, managed to hear scraps of conversation in between the calls:

"Quite a brawl, what?"

"You need plenty of wind for these things . . . ought to be held on a windy night."

"Now *duck* for the oyster—and *dive* for the clam!" shouted the caller. "One from the happy land . . . and everybody swing!"

Her hair was flying, her skirt was flying, her eyes bright.

People she knew passed and were gone, were met with, hands clasped, and passed on to the next group.

"Good way to reduce, if you ask me, or didn't you?"

"I could have reduced *her* to a pulp . . . but she quit talking before I got good and mad."

"Who does she think she is, anyhow?"

"Oh, she's new here."

"Is that an excuse?"

Color was high in Sue's cheeks. They were talking about her. She felt her mouth stretched in a grin, her hands were clammy.

"Swing the lady across the hall. . . ."
"Swing her high, don't let her fall. . . ."

"Some people never know when to quit, do they?"

"Why did David introduce her then? He could have shut her off."

"I hate gals who try to stir things up. . . . Gosh, didn't we all work? Why the extra credits for *some*?"

It seemed to her that she was always catching a remark like that. Did they know she heard? Did they mean her to, or didn't they care?

Maybe she *had* said too much. She remembered Judy's 'It isn't done here.' Apparently there were quite a few things that weren't 'done here.' Why hadn't David stopped her, if that was the case? In fairness, she realized that he had tried to stop her, but she had insisted on going on, doing things her way.

"Swing your partners!"

Sam swung her, and she felt dizzy. "Hey," he said,

pulling her at arm's length, "you're glassy-eyed! Getting winded?"

"My wind's all right," she returned. "It's in my mind."

He laughed. "I'd rather have a weak brain than weak feet this night."

The only thing that kept her going was that several people spoke to her about the dance itself. She and David had done a grand job; they were having a swell time . . . they ought to have these oftener. It helped; it made her feel less a pariah, more like one of them again.

Sam saw her home. He plodded wearily beside her through the brisk night. "It was fun while it lasted," he told her, hiding an enormous yawn. "Only trouble was, it lasted too long for this fellow. Guess I'm getting old. All I wanted to do there toward the last was curl up on one of those piles of hay . . . but then I remembered they were rented and I'd probably be carted off with them."

"Maybe you ate too many doughnuts," she suggested, but he scoffed at that. "I'm the doughnut champion of Brookhaven High," he said loudly. "And dough-nut contradict me."

She groaned appreciatively. Then, turning to him suddenly she said, "Sam, tell me something straight out. What did you think about tonight?"

"It was a wingeroo," he said with such sincerity that she smiled in the dark.

"No, I mean—what I said."

"What did you say?"

"My speech," she said with impatience.

"I wasn't listening . . . some late guys were still coming in at the door and a couple of 'em had no tickets."

"Some people didn't like it," she said.

"Some people don't like anything," he returned lazily. "Forget it."

It was comfort of a kind. She knew very well that he had heard it, but he wasn't going to rake it over. Forget it. Perhaps that was the best plan. The dance itself had been a huge success; she had been partly responsible for that fact . . . and she would be remembered for that as well as for her speech.

Getting into bed quietly she lay staring up into the dark. After a bit, as her eyes grew accustomed to the dimness, a faint light appeared and in it the leafless branches of the apple tree threw a moving pattern on her wall. She thought, half sleepily, maybe that's the way it is. When I get accustomed to things there will be a little more light; and a pattern will emerge. She hoped she hadn't spoiled the pattern tonight. She rolled over, put a hand under her cheek and closed her lids. A conviction rose in her, grew strong. The speech itself may have been wrong, but the feeling that had prompted her to make it was right. Very right.

6.

She went about for the next few days in a state of unpleasant expectancy. Remembering the remarks she had
heard at the dance, she was prepared for an avalanche of
criticism from her schoolmates. She almost found herself
going around with her shoulders drawn up tensely, and
she thought, But that's silly. I had a right to do what I did,
and they have a right to say what they think. She was prepared for them; she knew what she would answer if they

spoke to her critically; she spent quite some time rehearsing the various possibilities as she walked to and from school.

But no one said anything. It was a kind of anti-climax. Not that she wasn't grateful for their indifference. Even to her heightened perception they seemed about as usual—casual, friendly, and generally immersed in their own affairs. Quite a number of people spoke to her, in passing, about the dance. "Swell stuff," they said. "Quite a night." . . . "You put on a shindig, all right. I'm lame yet."

And no one said anything otherwise. Not even David. For that she was most grateful of all. And if he didn't, why should she bring it up? He had done as she requested, she had had her chance to make her speech—however ill-advised it may have been in his opinion—and that was all there was to it. The episode was over, so far as he and the others were concerned, it seemed. She was glad that she could consider it over, too. What had she accomplished by it? Nothing, perhaps, she thought ruefully. Except that she had made a point with herself. She had done something that she felt must be done. Let that be her satisfaction. And now to go on as before.

The next important thing in her life was the Glee Club concert. The dance was a thing of the past; everyone was busy now with some club, or game, or class project. The Glee Club, Miss Haynes had announced, would give its first concert the first week in December and she wanted no absenteeism except for the most bona fide reason. She expected everyone to work and work hard and to make this the finest concert the school had ever had.

"The only trouble with that is," Edna Wagner said in a sibilant whisper, turning to Sue, "Miss Thwaite expects you to work hard over Geom. and Miss Ringwood to work hard over History III, and Mr. Gregory to work hard over—"

"Will you repeat that for the benefit of the rest of us?" Miss Haynes inquired.

Edna colored to the roots of her hair. "It—it wasn't anything," she muttered.

"Dear me, do you mean to say you talk about nothing? Such a waste of time. Do let us hear so that we can judge for ourselves."

Edna, cornered, repeated her remarks so quickly that the words all ran together.

Miss Haynes gave a laugh, but not with much humor. "At least you seem to have got the general idea. Naturally every teacher expects you to work hard over his or her particular subject. I have no special concern with the rest of them, but I do know that I mean it for my particular project, and that's the forthcoming concert. If you don't care to work hard over this, too, Edna, you can always withdraw."

Edna managed to mumble something to the effect that she preferred to stay and, behind her music, rolled her eyes drolly at Sue. Oh, Miss Haynes was a martinet all right, Sue decided. But she didn't mind that. She rather liked a teacher who thought her special field was the most important of all and demanded your full attention and effort.

And there was no denying that Miss Haynes drew it out

of them! She lived and breathed music, and her ideas about how a thing should be rendered were vivid and compelling. She left them in no doubt about how a song should be sung.

"Think what you're singing," she would cry, in a sort of subdued fury that was more startling than a loud voice would have been. "Think, think! What you have in your mind colors your voice, don't you realize that?"

After they had done the phrase over again she wheeled around on the piano stool. "No, no! Who's saying this? A man, a young man. He's telling about his true love. He thinks there's no one like her in the world; he's trying to tell someone how beautiful she is, how sweet, how wonderful. How can he make this person understand? He puts his whole heart in his voice. . . . Close your eyes and imagine how he would feel, how he would put feeling into his words. Sing with your eyes closed now, and make your voice tender and sweet and thrilling. . . . Ah, that's better! That's more like it!"

Miss Haynes had chosen an interesting program for them to do . . . a group of folk songs of different nations, a group of early English songs, and a group of Christmas songs. Various members of the Glee Club were heard to mutter a bit in disapproval of one song or another, but on the whole they were enthusiastic about Miss Haynes' choices and worked enthusiastically on the forthcoming concert.

Sue found the Club relaxing. After a day's battling with Math. and History, English Comp. and Civics, she liked to go into the plain, sunny room and sing. It didn't matter what . . . she just enjoyed singing. Her ear was uncritical, but she had her favorites; some music 'did things' to her, as she said, and whenever she heard Beth's voice rising above the others, or when Beth practiced her solo part in several of the numbers, Sue knew a kind of ecstatic pleasure. She and Beth were to do the soprano and alto duet in "A Legend" by Tchaikowsky, and Sue felt as if she had a special privilege. The words that Katherine Davis had made for the great master's music stayed in her mind for days each time after she had sung them:

Christ, when a child, the legend goes,
A garden made with many a rose,
Tending the flowers with gentle care
That he might weave a crown to wear.

And when the flowers were all a-bloom,
To view the sight the children come,
Strip every branch with noisy scorn,
And leave the garden bare and torn.

"Now what is left to crown you here?"
The rogues called out with scornful jeer.
"There are the thorns left for me—
They'll make a crown," so answered he.

Then did they weave each naked stem
And crowned him with a diadem;
All pierced with thorns, his fair young head,
So stained with blood, like roses red . . . like roses red.

Beth's voice was like a rose, Sue thought, rich and warm and beautiful. Miss Haynes worked to have them sing together so that neither voice was too dominant, but Sue was so entranced listening to Beth that she found herself dwindling off and singing as quietly as possible so that she could hear the sensuous, simple beauty of the voice beside her.

"Between that song and *'I wonder as I wander,'* " Sue said ruefully one day, "I shall go mad! They haunt me . . . don't they you?"

"Yes," Beth said, in her friendly way. "They're so simple and real. That Appalachian folk song, to me, is just about perfect. Somebody wrote that who felt it from the heart . . . like some of the spirituals."

Sue nodded. "I know. I think we do it just about best of all, too. Probably because it's so simple that the feeling gets across to us." She walked a few steps in silence.

"Isn't it queer," she said then, her voice ruminative, "how you don't have to know an experience yourself to appreciate it? I mean . . . well, like these songs. The feeling is there in them, and it makes you feel, too. My heart nearly bursts with pity in the 'Legend' one—though it's something that never happened or could happen to me—"

"But it could," Beth said. "To some. It happened to Him, and it still happens, in a way, to others."

"I know what you mean," Sue said. "I put it wrong. I guess what I was trying to say was that if a thing is felt strongly enough, it doesn't matter how foreign it is to your life . . . it makes an impression. . . . And a good thing, too!" she laughed a little. "There are so many experiences a person—like me, or you—never has, and yet, in a way, you *can* have them, because somebody wrote about them in a way to get under your skin."

Beth gave her a sidelong glance of understanding. "They say that's what art is," she said quietly.

They had come out on the High School steps. It was a gray, chilly day, with an overcast sky and a mist in the air. Sue shifted her armload of books and rummaged in her purse.

"Oh, darn!" she cried. "I forgot my list! I made it out in Chem. today—I was afraid I'd forget some of the thousand and one things I want to buy downtown. . . . I haven't even begun on my Christmas shopping yet. I'll chase back and get it."

"I'll run along," Beth said quickly. "I have to get some stuff to put in Hank's box . . . we're late as it is, but we did send one off a couple of weeks ago that will be his Christmas one. . . . Only there were some other things I wanted to send him."

Sue thought, I hope I haven't hurt her. I didn't mean it that way. But of course she could have taken it to mean that I didn't want to walk with her again . . . waiting till we got outside and then saying I had forgot my list. I wouldn't have done it for the world if I thought— It was careless of me, but Beth must realize I'm not *that* much of a moral coward.

How silly the whole thing was! She enjoyed talking to Beth; she would talk to her whenever she felt like it, and walk with her, too, for that matter.

She rummaged blindly in her home-room desk and came up finally with the crumpled shopping list. How awkward life was sometimes! She could hurry and catch up with Beth, or she could wait till she was well out of sight. She stared down at the list. Under 'Kenny' was Airplane parts . . . Bicycle basket . . . Dog. He'd probably get the bicycle basket, but what he really wanted was the dog. I can't catch Beth now; I don't even know where she's gone. Oh surely, Beth wouldn't think harshly of her!

I'll see her tomorrow, Sue thought, and tell her— No, I will say nothing. I'll *show* her by my attitude that it was the way I said it was.

Just the same, she found it hard to concentrate on her shopping and had little success with it. It seemed to her that, early though it was, the things had been fairly well picked over, and what she saw was too high priced for her budget.

She wandered home finally, in a disspirited mood, chilled and unsatisfied, and was met at the door by her mother who announced acidly that the Garritys would be the death of her—now they had had a bonfire. So near the hedge which was the boundary between their properties that the hedge had caught fire and she'd had to telephone the fire department. They had just left and there was a big hole in the hedge. "And," said Mrs. Trowbridge, "my temper's ready to flame up, too. They said they didn't know the wind was in this direction! I really think they haven't their full complement of brains!"

"If we'd had a dog," Kenny said hopefully, "he could have been a watchdog and barked as soon as the fire started and then—"

"It was bad enough keeping *you* out of the fire," his mother said, "without having to watch a watchdog, too!"

"Mom," he persisted, "I saw a dog yesterday, just the kind I want. He liked me, too. I don't know what kind he was—maybe he was a couple of kinds—but Jim said if you go—"

"Kenny, I'm in no mood to discuss dogs right now. Have you cleaned out the cellar? A fire like that makes one realize how easily a thing can start if you're careless."

"Yes'm, I did. Gosh, Mom, I keep thinkin', if I save my money, and if I could earn some—"

Mrs. Trowbridge gave a brief smile. "You could earn some, I'm sure, but if you could save it is a question in my mind."

"But if I could, Mom, if I could, a dog—"

"Kenny, no more, please. You have two bunnies now, and a turtle, and a couple of fish."

"But a dog. . . ."

"A dog would be just something else for me to take care of." Kenny went off, mumbling darkly to himself, and Mrs. Trowbridge sighed. "A one-track mind, if ever I saw one. And it's generally a track I wish he weren't on."

Sue sympathized with Kenny's frustration, but she said nothing. If Kenny were a little older and wiser he would have realized that it was an inopportune moment to bring up the subject and would have waited. But Sue had her own problems, and she dismissed Kenny and his from her mind.

She didn't see Beth next day. Being in different classes made it difficult to come together, and after a day or two it seemed foolish to hunt her up for the express purpose of explaining her tactless behavior. She didn't meet Beth until the next Glee Club rehearsal and then Beth was the same as ever, to Sue's relief, and Miss Haynes put them through a grilling rehearsal and kept them so late that they all scattered for home as soon as it was over.

Sue had two tickets for her family, but Kenny, on the night of the concert, announced that he wasn't going. He'd sold his for fifty cents, and was planning to use the money for Christmas, he said. He had presents to buy, he said virtuously, and anyhow, who wanted to go and listen to a lot of old singing? He heard enough just with Sue warbling around the house the way she did.

Mrs. Trowbridge was upset because that meant she would have to stay home. Their father was still away, and she would not countenance Kenny being in the house alone. "And I did so want to hear it!" she said wistfully.

Kenny looked stricken and manfully said, well, if that was the way she felt about it, he'd go. But that was out of the question, too, for there was only a certain number of tickets and they had all been disposed of. There was scant chance of picking one up at the last moment.

Sam had offered to call for her, but she had to go early for a last-minute run-over and warm-up, and he said then that he would see her home. The Glee Club members were all dressed alike, in choir robes borrowed from various churches in town, and Miss Haynes insisted on their changing robes so that the variety of colors would harmonize and be in groups instead of giving a spotty effect. She was as nervous as an impresario, but confident of them. "Think of the music, not of me," she said. "If you think of the music, that will take care of me, too."

Sue was sorry her mother had to miss the concert, for the music was so beautiful and she wanted her to hear Beth. But she had so much to be thankful for, she thought, looking out over the sea of faces in the brightly lighted auditorium, and she sang from a full heart. Her duet with Beth went over beautifully, and she thrilled at the way it was received. It was Beth's voice that had carried it . . . and the dark face glowed with a kind of ecstasy as the notes soared and melted into the hall.

Miss Haynes' face was flushed with pleasure at the success of her first concert with the group. "You were splendid, all of you," she said. "There are a couple of things that need smoothing out, but I'll take those up at the next rehearsal. Meanwhile, I hope you'll all have a fine holiday. I want the a cappella group to stay behind, please . . . that is, all except Beth Varley. I want to talk to you."

They had done something wrong, perhaps, Sue thought, slipping out of her robe and folding it neatly in the box labeled First Presbyterian Church from which it had come. Miss Haynes was going to take them over the rails gently, before they went out, too puffed up with success.

Miss Haynes was waiting for the seven girls in the music room. She came to the point at once. "Something quite thrilling has come up," she announced. "A nice compliment to you. Mrs. Gerald Lowe—you know, she's chairman of the music department of the Women's Club here—has asked me as a special favor if you girls can come and give a small concert at the club for their Christmas meeting. Of course it will mean a little extra rehearsal, but not too much since it's all fresh, and we'll have to re-arrange some of our numbers. But it's such a nice compliment to us I do think we should do it, if you're willing. It would only be a half hour, and you'd all stay to tea afterward, she said."

There was a pleased hum among the girls and then Edna Wagner said, "But when would it be, Miss Haynes? I might have a date—"

"The twentieth," their teacher said. "That's the day school closes for Christmas vacation, as I'm sure you're well aware. Can you all make it?"

After a bit of consultation they agreed they all could make it. "I'll see about borrowing the robes again," Miss Haynes said, "and make out the program. Mrs. Lowe said they would have printed programs and I must get it to her at once. I'll see about getting Leslie Shaw to fill in, too. I hope she can do it. . . . Well, that's all for the moment. Thank you for staying on so I could settle the matter. You can run along now."

Sue heard, with a kind of delayed action, Miss Haynes' words repeating themselves in her mind. 'I'll see about getting Leslie Shaw to fill in.' It took her a full moment to realize what it implied. Leslie Shaw was a contralto. Miss Haynes meant that she should fill in for Beth. Had any of the others realized what Miss Haynes meant? Perhaps she herself had misunderstood.

Deliberately, and in a kind of numbness, she waited for the others to go.

"Miss Haynes—"

"Oh, you still here? Did you want something?" The voice was bright and friendly.

Sue said directly, "What happened to Beth? Did she say she couldn't do it?"

"No."

The answer was so brief and non-committal that it shocked Sue. She persisted.

"Do you mean she didn't want to?"

"I didn't ask her." The voice was not quite so friendly now; there was a chilly edge to it. Miss Haynes was busy with stacks of music, her hands efficiently dividing and stacking and re-sorting.

Sue came closer; her face was troubled. "But the octet won't be nearly the same without her—"

"Leslie Shaw, I'm sure, will be able to do it."

"I mean," Sue said anxiously, "Beth's voice *makes* the alto section. She's the singer of the lot . . . we all know that."

"Leslie will do well enough."

"But, Miss Haynes, *why* not Beth, when she's so wonderful?"

Miss Haynes stopped her sorting and faced around. "Are you interrogating me, Sue?"

"Well—well, you see, I want to understand. I should have thought *she'd* be more important than anyone. Especially if you want to make a good impression at the Women's Club."

"I am not compelled to give you reasons for my decision, Sue, but it may interest you to know that Mrs. Lowe expressly requested that I make a substitution."

Sue digested that for an unpleasant moment and found it too distasteful to assimilate. She said in astonishment,

"But there's the Supreme Court decision! People can't go against that!"

"They can and they do," said Miss Haynes. "A good many people still make their own personal decisions, as you must know from reading the papers."

Sue said, "You mean—"

"I mean," said Miss Haynes briskly, "that Mrs. Lowe realized, as I do, and as you may, if you give it some thought, that Beth Varley might have found it uncomfortable to be the sole Negro not only in the singing group but in the whole club. There will be about five hundred women there, I imagine."

Sue felt a flame of anger shoot through her. "Oh, Miss Haynes, you know that's not so! Beth wouldn't mind a bit —she loves to sing; singing is all that matters, not where she does it or for whom." She heard her voice rising shrilly and couldn't help it. "And as for the others, they—they ought to be ashamed of themselves!"

Miss Haynes obviously was trying to contain her temper. She bit her lip before she answered. "I am remembering, Sue, that you are young—and impetuous—and certainly without a very wide worldly knowledge. Believe me when I say that this is for the best. What's more, however you feel about it, it has been decided, and I think quite rightly."

"But *Beth* sang with *us*—"

"In school and with three other Negroes in the choir. This is entirely different. And, may I remind you again, the arrangement was at Mrs. Lowe's request."

"But you could have refused!" Sue cried hotly.

"I could," Miss Haynes said icily, "but I agree with her. And now, please, let's have no more. I think I've been entirely too long-suffering as it is. I'm tired . . . and perhaps your excuse is that you are, too. At any rate, good-night now."

Sam appeared in the doorway. "Uh, excuse me, Miss Haynes. They told me Sue was here. . . . I've been waiting, but that's all right; I'll be right down the hall."

Sue faced Miss Haynes, her eyes flashing. "Miss Haynes—"

"Good-night, I said."

"You won't ask Beth to be one of the eight?"

"I've told you my decision."

"Then," said Sue, her voice quivering and almost breaking, to her annoyance, "then I won't, either."

Miss Haynes whirled at that. "You've already agreed!"

"I know . . . but I didn't know what I was agreeing to. I won't sing with the group. It's unfair and . . . and horrid. If Beth's out, so am I!"

7.

Sam, piloting her by the elbow, said, "What's the matter—you cold?"

"No."

"You're trembling."

"I'm furious."

"What happened? I thought something was up . . . didn't you notice how I beat it out of there? Haynes looked like a stream of fire would come out of her nostrils, and you were flashing sparks like a wireless set."

When she told him, he let out a long, slow whistle. "Brother! You've done it, all right. In the army that would be called insub—insubor—"

"Insubordination," she shot back. "But this isn't the army. This is Brookhaven High. And Brookhaven. And America."

"Well, don't bite *my* head off, or who will see you home?"

She said, troubled, "But you can see how I feel, can't you, Sam?"

He gave a little laugh without much mirth in it. "I sure can! And I must say it looks sort of uncomfortable." When she did not reply, he said, "She a friend of yours?"

"Well, not exactly. I hardly know her. I'd *like* to know her better. But it isn't that. It's the *idea* of the thing."

"Give it time; it'll probably work itself out."

"How can it?" she demanded. "It's already been done."

"You're going to have an awful life," he commented, "if you get so steamed up about things."

She whirled on him. "Wouldn't you?" she asked fiercely. "Wouldn't you get—steamed up, if you thought something was wrong, or it hurt?"

He considered for a moment. "Sure, if I thought it would help. But how does this help?"

"I—don't know."

"You've just made matters worse, so far as I can see. Busted up the octet, or whatever you call it, and made Haynes mad, and maybe even Beth Varley won't thank you. Don't see why she should, in fact."

"I don't expect her to," she said with spirit. "And you know very well that isn't why I did it."

"Sure . . . sure," he soothed. "Say, do we have to talk about this all the way home?"

Sue said contritely, "I'm sorry, Sam. I know I sound cross and—hateful, but I can't just let it drop. I did what I did out of temper, maybe . . . but there was something underneath. I felt it was all wrong of Miss Haynes to have given in that way—"

"What else could she have done?"

"She could have said, 'My group will sing as a group or not at all.' "

"She could have," he agreed. "But maybe she didn't see it that way."

"But that's it!" Sue cried, in exasperation. "What other way is there to see it? Beth Varley has the most beautiful voice of anyone in the group. To leave her out was a—a kind of insult. What does it matter whether a person is Chinese or Negro or white or has red hair or green or black? The only way I could show how I felt was to get out, too."

She could sense that he was grinning. "Well, you're out all right. What I wonder about is whether you'll get back in."

Words crowded to her lips but she bit them back. If Sam disappointed her somewhat, it wasn't his fault. He didn't mean to be cruel. That was the way he looked at things—the way most of their classmates looked at it, for that matter, she thought.

Forget it, he had said that other time. And it had seemed good advice then. *But how does this help?* he was saying now. He didn't think what she had done had any meaning, other than to make trouble for herself and possibly for Beth. He thought that she should have let matters ride—that they would have smoothed out in the course of time. How could they? Why shouldn't you try to do something if you felt strongly about it? Why shouldn't you voice your disapproval in the only way you could voice it—by your own actions?

Maybe it wouldn't help. Pondering it in the cold light of day, she came to that doubtful point, too. Maybe it would only make trouble, and that was the last thing she aimed for. The gang thought she was rather odd even now. How would they look on this newest outburst? It was queer . . . this was the last sort of thing she had envisioned for herself when she came to Brookhaven. Things had started out so wonderfully, too . . . taken in by the very ones whom she most wanted to have like her; given important jobs; growing friendship with her classmates; a snug berth in the coveted Glee Club. . . . What was she jeopardizing it all for?

She could forget it, as Sam had advised on that other occasion. She could go on as if nothing had happened; she could turn up at Glee Club, and make a tacit apology to Miss Haynes. She could try to forget the whole unpleasant incident, and everyone else would, too, and she could go on as before. Or could she?

No, she knew she couldn't. That was a physical, a mental, impossibility now. The thing had happened, and by happening, it had done something to her. If she forgot the incident and acted as if nothing had happened, she would be doing herself a real harm.

Unconsciously, she sighed. It would have been pleasant to go on as before. But how long would it have lasted? If not this, then something else might have occurred that would have roused her to action of a sort . . . as this had done. And then she would have had to decide, too, whether she would let it pass or be true to her convictions.

It would have been hard to know, Sue decided afterward, what she would have done, if it hadn't been for Kay Hamilton. She was what the papers described invariably in their headlines about her as a 'local author.' Brookhaven was proud of her, in its way, and Sue had been awed to discover that she was a resident of the town. For Kay Hamilton's books were invariably on her reading list. She borrowed them at the rental library and the Public Library—when she could find them in. Now Kay Hamilton was to talk to them in morning Assembly. She wondered what she was like . . . it was disconcerting sometimes, she gathered, to meet authors face to face; you had built up an idea of them and when you saw them —in life or in a photograph—it was apt to be disillusioning.

She stood now, during the closing bars of "America the Beautiful" and tried to picture what the author would be like. She wrote enchantingly and forcefully of problems that young people met. Did she know how to meet problems in her own life? Or was she so fortunately placed that she didn't have them—at least not the kind you lost sleep over?

Bob Grossman, president of the Student Council, introduced her. He seemed a little awed, himself, because he stumbled over the facts of her life, forgot part of his prepared speech, and gave the titles of her two latest novels wrong. Miss Hamilton stepped onto the stage.

Sue felt let down. She was a plain woman . . . average height, brown hair tinged with a wing of gray, unfashionable clothes . . . good, no doubt, but nothing striking. The feeling of disappointment was only momentary, however, for when she began to speak, you forgot what she looked like. Her voice was clear and fresh and warm, and an elusive dimple played around her humorous mouth. It was quite startling. She spoke directly at her audience, and Sue had the sensation that she was the only one being addressed, so personal and vital was the voice.

"Every time I stand up here," she said, "I wonder what I can say that will be worth your listening. I remember how I used to feel when I sat where you're sitting now— if you can imagine that I was ever that young. I used to hope that words of wisdom would fall from the lips of the sere and ancient celebrity addressing us . . . some sort of magic formula that would make everything clear and . . . and easy.

"Bob says that you want to know what makes an author tick; how I came to be such an odd creature in the first place. I don't mind telling you, though it's nothing new and I've had no thrilling adventures, because I know that I used to want to know that sort of thing, too."

And she told them, in offhand, humorous fashion, how her career had started and some of the amusing things that had happened in the course of her successful life. "But when it comes right down to it, this may make interesting chitchat, but it doesn't help you one little bit.

"What matters in making an author—and in making any other person—is what he thinks and what he says and what he does. And why. What he believes, and therefore how he acts.

"What you are as an individual is what matters. Right now, I know, dressing like your contemporaries and doing what they do and going where they go and talking the way they talk is terribly important. And that's all right . . . up to a point. It's human nature to shun being different. People are gregarious; they enjoy being with others, and to be with others you have to be sufficiently like them to fit in."

She illustrated her point with some telling examples—the current craze in dress for boys and girls, some of their pet expressions heard on every side; the popularity of certain juke spots and movie idols and records.

"The trouble with being like everyone else," Miss Hamilton went on, leaning over the lectern in her casual fashion, "is that it gets to be a habit. It's an insidious habit . . . it starts with innocuous things like dress, and it creeps over you until you're acting and thinking like everyone else, too. No matter whether it's right or wrong. Just because it's easiest."

Sue felt herself sitting straighter. This was coming down her alley. Was there something special for her here?

"Dare to be different!" the speaker's voice rang out with earnestness. "If there's something you want to do, and it's right and best for you—whether others are doing it or not—go ahead and do it! If you believe in a thing, work for it—whether others believe or not. By your belief and your work you can change *them*. By changing one person, you may change the world. But by being true to yourself and your beliefs you will grow, and achieve the status of a true adult. An 'adult' being one who knows what's right, and what is honorable. Nowadays when so much depends on individual thought and effort, you have to be surer than ever that what you do and say is done and said because it's your actual conviction . . . something you've reasoned out for yourself and are ready to stand up and fight for—if it comes to that.

"Even if you don't want to be a leader—for that's what leaders are made of—you certainly don't want to be a follower all your days; a rubber-stamp—a yes-woman or yes-man—a voice that is always lost in the chorus. There must always be a first. Florence Nightingale was a first; Sister Kenny and George Washington Carver; Lillian Gilbreth and Albert Schweitzer and Mary Bethune. It isn't always easy, but it's the only way you'll justify your existence and acquire a true measure of happiness. Be an individual . . . dare to be different!"

Afterwards, moving slowly down the corridor in a turgid stream, the comments flew thick and fast.

"She 'dared to be different,' all right! Did you see her *shoes*?"

"And the way she wore her hair. Hasn't changed it, I bet, since graduation."

"She had a nice voice, though."

"She must make plenty. . . . I wish I had what she makes a year."

"She certainly doesn't look it!"

"Who's this Mary Bethune she talked about? Never heard of her." That was Edna Wagner, crowding closer to Sue. "What did she do? Do you know?"

"No," Susan said thoughtfully. "I wonder. . . . I'll have to find out."

"Oh well," Judy said airily, "who cares? Probably something awfully stuffy and good. I was disappointed. I like Hamilton's books, but I thought she'd tell us more about herself, and how she got that way."

"She did," Sue said. "By being different."

Judy hooted. "Different! Mother thinks I act queer half the time as it is. What she wants is for me to be more normal, she says. . . . Well, here's where I go to the slaughter. 'Bye."

Was that all the impression Kay Hamilton had made on them? Or were they hiding something, even from themselves? Because, for her, it had been a revealing talk. It had stirred her; it had put new strength into her. She thought, It's almost as if she knew what was troubling me and was talking to *me*.

If you believed in something, Miss Hamilton had said. If you felt it was right—even though no one else did—you had to stand up for it; fight for it if necessary. That applied to her, didn't it? That way you measured up to yourself; you were an individual, not part of a herd. You were true to yourself. She didn't want to fight . . . she didn't want things to be unpleasant or hard. But it had gone beyond what she wanted. It had touched something deep in her, something she believed in, and she had done what she felt was right.

She wished she could have had a little talk with Miss Hamilton. But perhaps that wasn't necessary at all. She had really said everything necessary in those few minutes, when you came down to it. The rest was up to herself.

Susan came upon Beth Varley unexpectedly near her locker that afternoon. She went up to her. But Beth spoke first.

"I heard . . . about your leaving the Glee Club," she said directly.

"Yes."

"You did it—because of my not being asked?"

"Yes," Sue said again, answering as candidly as Beth was asking.

Beth took out her coat and slipped into it slowly. Her eyes were on Sue's, and they were warm, but serious.

"I'm sorry."

"I'm not."

"I mean," Beth said, "I'm sorry if it spoils things for you. I'm terribly grateful for what you did—for me. But you see, I don't honestly care too much about this."

Sue looked at her in surprise.

"Oh, it hurts . . . things like that are bound to hurt, no matter how often they happen. You never get really used to it. But in this case I *don't* mind too much, because I've been asked to sing at the church—our church—for a special program Christmas week, and I'm going to need every spare minute to practice."

"Oh, that's wonderful!" Sue cried. She was very happy about it. It just seemed to have happened at the right time. Not that this changed the situation any, but it must help Beth to have something else to think about now, and to plan for. "What are you doing?"

"Some old Christmas songs, I think, and a group of spirituals. I can't quite make up my mind; I'll see what the minister says, and then it will depend on the time I have. I'll have to fit things in."

"I'd love to hear you!" Sue said impulsively.

"Would you?" Beth smiled in appreciation. "Why don't you come, if you can? It will be crowded . . . it's Christmas Eve, but there'd always be room. I'd ask Mother to save a seat for you."

"Where is it to be?"

"At our church—Mt. Zion. You know—or perhaps you don't—it's between Highland and Forsythe, on Ninth Street. You couldn't miss it; it's set up high and has three colored glass windows on either side of the main door."

"I'd love to come," Sue repeated. "And of course I know where that is."

"You've no idea," Beth said, her voice lowering, "how much it means to me. What you did. Perhaps I never should have gone into the Club in the first place. . . ."

"No!" Sue said sharply. "Don't think that. You belong there. I did what I did because I wanted to."

"I know," Beth said. "But it shouldn't have been necessary." She said it calmly, in deep seriousness.

"That's it," Sue nodded. "The whole thing was wrong." She paused, and a thought struck her. "D'you know, Beth, I don't think Miss Haynes was too happy about it, either. Or she wouldn't have been so cross."

8.

"It was ghastly!" Edna told her dramatically, when they met downtown the day after the concert at the Women's Club. A Salvation Army lass was ringing her bell beside the swinging black pot; children were gazing wide-eyed at a rotund Santa Claus stationed at the corner; and people were scurrying along, heads bent against the wintry wind that whipped flurries of snow into fitful gusts. Edna pulled Sue into the lee of a store entrance and rubbed her red nose. "I'm frozen, and I can't find a thing that I can afford. . . . You should have been there in the gallery—it was a complete flop!"

"Well, tell me!"

"What is there to tell? Everybody knew it *would* be, with Leslie Shaw having to step in, and you stepping out. She scarcely knew her notes and kept her head down in her book all the time, and what's more, in her couple of solo passages she flatted twice and you could actually see Haynes gritting her teeth! The 'Noel, Noel' sounded like a cat's party, with all the cats feeling sort of sick . . . and that Appalachian song you're so crazy about—" she raised her hands and rolled her eyes—"well, it was pitiful. Everything was so *thin* without you two good voices, and the women weren't one little bit pleased. They fidgeted and raised their eyebrows and rustled their programs. And afterwards!"

"Afterwards?"

"At the tea. They didn't hesitate to say what they thought, in a sort of well-bred fashion—you know, 'Did some of you girls have dreadful colds? It didn't sound quite right'—that sort of thing."

"I'm sorry," Susan said thoughtfully.

"You ought to be!" Edna said with vigor. "Letting us down like that! Of course the whole thing was a terrible nuisance, coming right on top of Christmas vac. and shopping and all—but we've got a black eye with that Club, and Miss Haynes is fit to be tied. There was a music critic there, too—you know, that man who does them for the Eagle—and he looked pained. I'll bet he lambastes us properly in tonight's paper. You can read it and gloat! Well, I've got to run. . . . Do you have any ideas what to give an elderly aunt who doesn't like books or candy or sweaters—something that costs no more than a dollar?"

Sue laughed. "I have not! What's more, I'd like a little help myself. See you in January!"

"If not sooner. You going to Anne's party?"

"No," Sue said. "I didn't know she was having one."

"Oops, my mistake. . . . Oh, well, you know her house is small—I imagine it'll be a crush. Merry Christmas!"

"Merry Christmas!"

So the club concert had been a flop. She had thought it might go rather badly, particularly without Beth's support, but she had not wished for it. That she could say honestly. It must have been a blow to Miss Haynes, and to have to meet the women's condescending disapproval must have been galling. Too, it would have been hard on the other girls . . . they had looked forward to the occasion and wanted it to go off brilliantly.

It was obvious, even from Edna's light-hearted remarks, that they would blame her largely for what had happened. It was queer that Edna had said nothing about missing Beth . . . they seemed to have taken that part as a matter of course. But that *she* should have stepped out too had made them angry. They felt that she had let them down. But she was not sorry she had done it . . . even if she did have to miss Anne's party.

That came as something of a shock. Of course Anne was entitled to ask anybody to her party whom she wanted to . . . and by the same token leave out anybody. But she knew that she would have been one of the invited guests

. . . if it hadn't been for the Glee Club affair. This was the crowd's way of saying that they didn't like what she had done. She wasn't one of them any more if she acted like that.

Sue walked on soberly. Well, what now? It was going to be hard to take. She would have loved Anne's party, and all the other things that the holidays would have offered. Was this what it meant to stand up and fight for what you believed in? If it was, it was just as hard as any pitched battle. You had to have a special kind of strength to meet the hurt and disappointment that came your way when you acted 'on the strength of your convictions,' as Miss Hamilton had said.

She shook her shoulders, brushed a snowflake out of her eye, and dropped a dime in the pot of the Salvation Army lass. The fun had gone out of her shopping; she might as well go home.

She heard voices as she entered the front door and tried to slip past the living-room and up the stairs to her room, but her mother called out,

"Come in, dear! Mrs. Kincaid is here."

Sue recognized a certain pleasurable excitement in her mother's voice. Mrs. Kincaid was head of the Women's Alliance at the church, and active in civic affairs. Sue realized how happy her mother must be to have this call.

Mrs. Kincaid was short and compact, with iron-gray hair and near-sighted eyes behind thick glasses. Sue went forward and greeted her and her clasp was friendly.

"Your mother tells me you like our town and your work at High School!"

"Oh yes!" Sue said warmly.

"We think we have one of the finest High Schools in the state," Mrs. Kincaid said with satisfaction. "In fact, we're rated that way. Such a nice group of young people, and good instructors. And there's so much going on. Are you in any of their activities?"

"She was co-chairman of the Junior-Freshman Hop," Mrs. Trowbridge put in proudly.

"I heard about that," Mrs. Kincaid said. "My daughter's child is a freshman; she said it was a most successful affair."

"And I belong to the Athletic Association and the Records Club and the Glee Club." She turned to her mother. "I'll fix some tea, shall I?"

"That would be very nice, dear. Use the blue cups. And perhaps you could make some cinnamon toast?"

"Leave it to me."

Susan could hear the undertone of their voices as she scurried about the kitchen getting the tea ready. They seemed to be getting along well together. When she brought in the tray Mrs. Kincaid beamed at her.

"So helpful! . . . I've been telling your mother that she ought to belong to our Women's Club. I'm not a member myself, but I could get one of our Alliance women to sponsor her. They have such interesting things most of the time." A thought struck her. "You said the Glee Club! Oh dear, I understood they put on a Christmas program there and it was a dreadful affair. So ill-prepared. Were you—that is, one hears such rumors, of course—were you in it and is it true?"

Sue said carefully, "Yes, it's true. But I wasn't there."

"I thought you said——" Mrs. Kincaid's voice trailed upward.

"I was supposed to be. But I refused." She passed Mrs. Kincaid the cream and sugar.

"Dear me!" their guest laughed. "Hoity-toity! Or temperamental, perhaps, or too near Christmas?" She put two heaping teaspoons of sugar and a liberal amount of cream in her tea, and began stirring, glancing up at Sue with a smile.

Mrs. Trowbridge nervously tried to change the subject. "There's always so much going on at this time of year. And I still haven't bought a tree. We must get downtown tomorrow at the latest, Sue, and choose one."

Mrs. Kincaid was not to be sidetracked. "You'll find plenty of bargains—picked over, of course, but suitable. Now do tell me why you weren't with your Glee Club . . . of course you can be glad you were away, if it was such a disappointment. The women tell me it was really dreadful; they were quite put out, after all they'd heard about Miss Haynes."

Susan said, "Miss Haynes trains us wonderfully. But she had picked eight girls to go to the Club . . . and she left out one of our very best voices, and when I heard that I refused to go, too, so they had to put in two others at the last minute."

"Well!" said Mrs. Kincaid, and stopped stirring. "I can imagine how Miss Haynes felt. What was the matter with the other girl?"

Mrs. Trowbridge was tapping her toe nervously on the floor; Susan knew that she wished the subject had never come up. But she had to answer. "She was a Negro," she said.

Mrs. Kincaid said, "So you didn't want to—Of course not—that is, I see."

She had misunderstood. Let it go at that. No, she couldn't. "I mean," she said distinctly, "that she was left out simply because she was a Negro, so I wouldn't sing, either."

Their guest's eyebrows rose a trifle; she set her tea-cup down carefully. "No doubt Miss Haynes was upset. Young people," she looked across at Sue's mother with a pitying smile, "*are* so difficult these days. Of course we all try to be Christian and all that, but it does seem a bit—well—"

What she would have said remained forever a secret. At that moment the front door banged and Kenny blew into the room, propelled by a small dirty white dynamo.

"Look, Mom, look! I got him! See? Isn't he a fella? He's got more pep than a tractor—pulled me all the way home."

"Kenny!" Laura Trowbridge was nearing the end of her rope. "We have a guest. This is my son, Kenneth, Mrs. Kincaid." Mrs. Kincaid smiled frigidly and Kenny shot a quick nod in her direction.

"Howjado . . . I got him for a dollar. The man at the pound let me have him if I'd give him a good home, and I told him—"

"Never mind that now. Take him out at once. He's filthy. And you're tracking snow all over the rug."

"He's smart as a whip. I kin tell. And he's house-broken, too, the man said. I can't understand why anybody'd give up a fella like this—"

"We'll discuss it later. I'm asking you now to take him out at once, and *leave* him out."

"Outside? It's cold. I could put him in the cellar." The rope slipped his fingers; the little eager dirty white dog lunged at Mrs. Kincaid who drew back in dismay, gathering her skirt close to her. The dog smelled the cinnamon toast, licked one off the plate with a quick red tongue, and sniffing around the edge of the table, proved conclusively that he was not house-broken.

"Kenny!" Spots of color rode painfully on Mrs. Trowbridge's cheekbones.

Susan rescued the pup and dragged him out of the room; Kenny perforce followed. "I'm gonna keep him, though," Kenny said doggedly. "I bought him; he's mine."

"I must be going," Mrs. Kincaid was heard to say. "So much to do. You have a lively household, I can see, Mrs. Trowbridge. Young people. . . ."

Mrs. Trowbridge came out into the kitchen carrying the tea-tray. "I've had quite enough," she said, her voice trembling. "I can just picture what that Mrs. Kincaid will say about us. I expressly said I did not want a dog around, Kenneth, and you—"

"He's all I want for Christmas!" Kenny wailed. "I'm gonna keep him. He only did that because he was excited. . . ."

"And you go and clean it up at once. Take that rag . . . and plenty of water."

Kenny disappeared, and Mrs. Trowbridge turned to her daughter. "As for you, Susan, it's unfortunate that you couldn't have let that topic drop. You know how I feel about the whole matter, and now Mrs. Kincaid will be spreading all over town that we—that we— What *is* there about this Beth Varley that has you so bemused? I wish you'd stop talking about her."

Susan knew it was the wrong moment to say it, but it came out. She felt badly, too, yet underneath was a core of determination in her. "She's asked me to come and hear her sing at her church."

"Well, you needn't go; that's simple."

"I want to go, though, Mom. Her voice is beautiful! If you could only hear it! It's to be a special program Christmas Eve—"

At that Mrs. Trowbridge wheeled angrily. "And Christmas Eve of all times! You know we'll all be busy trimming the tree! And getting ready for the next day. And who would take you? Not I!"

Sue thought rebelliously, Father would, if he were here! He wouldn't feel this way. She wished he did not have to be away so much; his very presence lent her strength. He was a gentle man, quiet, easy-going, tolerant. She was sure he would defend her position, perhaps make her feel stronger for his tacit support. But she was alone.

Her mother was still talking. "And I won't hear of you going into that neighborhood alone. I don't know what's come over you. Get out the things for supper. Not that I feel I could eat a bite."

9.

In the end, Kenny got his dog, but Sue did not get to go to Beth's recital.

The dog *was* ingratiating, with an appealing manner and melting brown eyes and one upright ear. Once his excitement had passed he proved to be fairly well-mannered and Kenny's rhapsodic face, when he was told that he might keep him—on condition that he take over his care and training—was compensation enough, Mrs. Trowbridge decided, for whatever commotion the dog might cause. Kenny promptly named him Bozo, scrubbed him white, bought him a collar, traded some stamps and marbles for an almost-new leash, and inveigled his father into helping him build a dog-house which, he said, Bozo would sleep in, outside, as soon as the weather was warmer.

Kenny, at least, was happy. But Sue, in spite of the general Christmas-y atmosphere pervading the house, had an uneasy feeling. While she helped bake the Christmas cookies and give the house its holiday slick-up, while she wrapped gifts and addressed cards and assisted her mother in all the happy preparations, she kept turning over in her mind what she should say to Beth. And how should she say it? Should she call her up or drop her a note? Should she simply wait till later and explain—in some fashion— why she had not come?

As it turned out, the decision was taken from her. She had talked to her mother, fruitlessly—risking her displeasure and annoyance—about the possibility of going. She could take a cab, Sue said. It would never do, her mother countered; how would she get home? She could go for just a little while, Sue suggested, so that at least she had put in an appearance. It wasn't that important, her mother told her, and since the whole idea was distasteful to her, she might as well drop it. For one thing, Mrs. Trowbridge said a bit acidly, Sue had brought this on herself by impulsively accepting an invitation which, on sober thought, she would have realized was out of the question.

Sue rebelled inwardly and vocally, but it did no good. She felt trapped and searched for some way of easing the situation. When she developed a sore throat it seemed like the answer to her predicament, but an answer which she scorned. The throat, however, became so raw that swallowing was difficult, and Doctor Marsh said she must stay in bed for a few days and he would drop in again. She gargled conscientiously and took the prescribed pills, so that she could be on hand for the Christmas festivities. Meanwhile she telephoned Beth and told her why she could not come.

Beth was sympathetic. "I'm sorry *you* have it," she said, "but oh, how glad I am *I* don't just at this particular time."

"So am I," Sue said warmly. "That's just one of the things that made me decide I wouldn't be a singer! . . . Have a wonderful time, Beth, and I wish I could be there!"

She thought, as she hung up the receiver, that settles this. But when something else comes up, what then? It was just a temporary solution, and she was not happy about it.

When she was better she stopped at the Library and hunted up material on Mary Bethune. The name had stuck in her memory since Kay Hamilton's talk, and she wondered about this woman who belonged with those who had had the courage to be 'first.' She knew about most of the others. It amazed her to discover that Mary McLeod Bethune was a Negro woman. Somehow she had never thought of that. And so, because of her concern over Beth, it took on added significance. She pored over the books and articles the librarian laid out for her, losing herself in the story of a life. An excitement coursed through her, mounting as she read. What spirit the woman had—what courage and faith!

She had been one of seventeen children born to ex-slaves and spent her childhood working from dawn to dark in the cottonfields. But she had had a dream. And that dream led her to an amazing career in education and humanitarianism. She had only a dollar and a half and her faith in God when she started a college for Negroes in Florida. She bought a dump-heap before she had any money, but by her determination and inspired 'begging,' as she called it, she raised building after building through the years. What began as a squalid shack where her children had to use charred splinters for pencils and packing boxes for seats and mashed elderberries for ink, became, through her efforts, Bethune-Cookman College valued at more than a million dollars.

She had done everything in the course of a long, full life. She had served her own people and battled against intolerance in the world; she had served as a consultant to the United Nations Conference and worked with educational leaders throughout the world. Presidents had received her, medals had been bestowed upon her, statesmen had come to see her. Sue gazed at the strong, kindly face, crowned with white hair, and marveled at how far she had come and how much she had done—because she believed it must be done, because she had felt called upon to do it. And she *had* done it, in spite of setbacks and ridicule and discouragement and lack of funds. Her people must be proud of her.

Sue amended that, with an almost guilty start. Not only *her* people . . . *all* people should be proud of her.

Every race had its great and good. How many there were that you didn't know about! And should. Men and women like George Washington Carver and Mary Bethune —and how many hundred others?—who worked with a vision and met defeat to triumph over it in the end. Who cared enough to do things that needed doing, no matter how the odds were against them.

She decided to make Mary Bethune the subject of her long theme, and wondered whether Miss McNellis would like that. If she could just go home and write it down, fired as she was with this new enthusiasm, it would be good. Perhaps she ought to begin it, anyhow, while she was 'all steamed up.'

Coming down the library steps she practically ran into Dave Grinnell. He put out a steadying elbow and caught her toppling pile of books.

"Hey," he grinned, "what is this, a busman's holiday? I thought you wouldn't want to have anything to do with books during vac."

She laughed up at him, "And what are *you* going to the Library for—a drink of water?"

He acknowledged the thrust with a feigned wince but he countered, "Just wanted to check up on how many other grinds there were in the Junior Class. Something should be done about it. . . . What have you got here?"

She told him. "And I'd never heard of her till Miss Hamilton mentioned her in her talk. Had you?"

"No," he said easily, "but that doesn't mean anything. There are millions of people I never heard of."

"She's marvelous!" Sue said vigorously. "I wish I could have met her."

"Why?"

"Well—" she spread her hands a little, "because she would have inspired me, I imagine."

"Not just because she was a Negro?" he asked, giving her a steady look.

She returned it, her voice surprised. "Of course not. What a funny thing to say!"

He came down a step, but he still towered over her. "Listen," he said earnestly. "Don't get me wrong. But you can't blame me—or any of us, I guess—for thinking you're pretty much on their side. The way you've acted; the things you've said. Why don't you champion your own kind, if you've got to be a missionary?"

She paused to arrange her thoughts and to get control of her tongue. "*You* listen," she said. "I'm not trying to be a missionary; I'm not on 'their' side against yours. I'd do the same for anyone—for Sam or Judy or you—if I thought you were having a bad deal. It's not fair of you to say things like that. It just happens that Beth Varley— and Fern and George, when it comes to that—are Negroes, but that's beside the point."

"Have it your own way," he said. "It's your battle, I guess. We thought you were an awfully nice kind when you came; only now—"

"Now?" she insisted.

"Well, you know how it is. If you go against the regular thing, if you insist on running things your way . . . it sort of makes people wonder, that's all. Maybe you can buck the herd, I don't know. I'm just telling you how it is."

Sue turned from him without another word. There were

too many things to say, and she didn't know how to say them. Walking away blindly, she was still aware that he was looking after her . . . almost as if he had wanted to go on, wanted *her* to go on. She was aware of her anger, and that she had a right to be angry. But she knew he was troubled or he would never have spoken as he did. Next time, she thought, I'll stay and have it out with him. Next time I'll be better prepared; if he can speak out, so can I. Only, the thought was a bleak one now, will there be a next time?

Maybe you can buck the herd, he had said. I don't want to buck the herd. I want to be like them, I want them to like me. They had liked her, he said—and she knew that from her own experiences—but if she was going to be 'different,' their liking would cool. It had already cooled.

Did Miss Hamilton know all this? Or was she just talking from a theory? It was all right to say things like that— they sounded fine and big and courageous and *right*—but when you had to live them, it was a more difficult matter, an altogether different business.

Maybe you can buck the herd. . . . That was David's way of saying it. But there were plenty of people who had actually done just that—bucked the herd. They had, in other words, dared to be different. Not because they wanted to, so much as because they had to. Something in them demanded it. They wouldn't have felt right otherwise.

She remembered some of the things she had just read about Mary Bethune. There were plenty of times when she might have been discouraged and given up . . . when people turned from her, when she was down to her last dollar and didn't know where the next was coming from, or when people disagreed with her or refused to help. She might have quit then . . . but she didn't. She believed so much in what she was doing that she had 'bucked the herd.' And eventually things had come right for her, and for those she wanted to help.

When school re-opened after Christmas vacation, Sue turned up at the first Glee Club rehearsal. It took some inner strength to do it. It would have been so easy to stay out, and nurse her grievance and her sense of righteousness. But it wouldn't help matters any, she supposed.

Miss Haynes seemed glad to see her, and in her brusque fashion told her to take her place, she had no time to waste, they must begin at once on their plans for the spring school concert.

"I have decided," she announced, looking straight ahead, "not to accept any outside engagements. We are not sufficiently prepared to take them on. After all, we are primarily a school group, and we will confine our singing to the school."

Beth smiled at her warmly, and afterwards Sue said, "How did *your* concert go?"

Beth's face lit up. "Oh, it was good, I think. Everybody seemed to be happy about it. Maybe it was just the Christmas spirit and because our people love to sing and love singing. . . . The children were sweet. They came marching up the aisle, from the littlest ones to the teen-agers, and their faces were shining, and their eyes, and they looked just like little angels!"

The phrase struck Sue. Little *brown* angels, she thought.

And why not? Why should you arrogate angels to your own race? Wasn't being 'angelic' a matter of spirit rather than color? She felt almost as if she had made a discovery. She turned to Beth.

"I wish I could have seen them," she said. "I can imagine how sweet they were."

The school curriculum seemed to take on added velocity with the new term. There was more work in each class, more intensified demands from teachers, and their own boning for 'mid-years.' Sue found herself involved in a round of study, club meetings and household chores, and the weeks flew by. She was anxious to keep her marks high because she wanted to go to college and she had hopes of getting a scholarship.

"Where are *you* going?" Gracie asked her one day when they were talking about colleges.

"I don't know," Sue said. "There's Radcliffe—"

"No campus."

"Or Smith—"

"Bluestocking; not as much so as Bryn Mawr, but def. bluestocking."

"And Wellesley—"

"I'd like to go *there* if anywhere," Gracie said. "Nice buildings, and near Boston and plenty of boys. But four more years of study? I don't think I could bear it. I'd prefer to marry early and go around the world a couple of times before I settle down and have three children—two boys and a girl."

"Your aims are high," Sue laughed, "if not intellectual. I think you're hardly college material."

"Well," Gracie said with complacence, "it takes all

kinds to make a world. Have you heard that before? And if I do have to go to college—my aunt went and she's sort of set on it and would help me through, if I got in in the first place—I really want to go to a co-ed one. No wasting *my* sweetness on the desert air! Anyhow, I think it would be much more interesting."

"Define 'interesting,' " said Judy, who had come up.

"*I* think," Sue put in, "that your best bet is to stay out."

"That's easy," Gracie said. "In fact, it's probably inevitable. I can't seem to make the necessary effort . . . and if I did go, how would I stay?"

"Let's ignore her," Judy advised. "She's a bad influence."

"We have to be strong enough to withstand her," Sue laughed. "I really want to go. . . . I've set my heart on it. It's just a matter of choosing which college, and getting the money for it."

"Scholarships help."

"But they're not all. And what's more, how do I know I'd get one, even a small one? Dad has some money set aside for me, but it's going to be a pull for four years. I'll have to work this summer and next." She thought a moment and amended that. "I *want* to work. It would be fun earning some of the money myself. The question is, at what? What kind of job could I get?"

"They always have jobs up on the bulletin board," Judy said. "But one look at them and you turn sort of faint. They aren't very exciting and they don't pay much."

"What do you expect?" Sue asked reasonably. "We aren't experienced, and we haven't any special training."

"I know," Judy sighed. "But do you have to be so sickening? I always keep hoping something will turn up like, 'Young woman wanted to take complete charge of office. No experience necessary. Good salary and five-day week.' "

"And what you get," Gracie supplemented, "is 'Baby-sitters. Fifty cents an hour.' Or 'Luncheonette needs waitress. No experience, but flat feet preferred.' "

They broke up, laughing, but Sue thought, It really isn't so funny. We want so much and have nothing—except maybe eagerness—to give. Why do we expect the world laid at our feet? Judy and Gracie talked that way because they liked to poke fun at things, and they didn't need jobs. Judy had already said they were going to the Lakes for six weeks, and Gracie's rich aunt had promised to take her on a motor jaunt through New England. But for herself. . . . Well, there would be no vacation away from home this year certainly. They were saving what money they could for another house, and she knew that her father was laying away regular sums for her college education and Kenny's. There was the new car to pay for, and her mother's new washing machine, and all the recent repairs to the house. Then, too, they needed to fix up the garage. No, there would be no vacation this year, unless they took a few week-end trips, and that would depend on her father's schedule.

It would have been fun to go away, but she didn't feel too badly about it. The thing was, if she had to have a job, she hoped it would be a good one, one that would repay her, in interest and funds, for working during the hot summer months. She made a mental note to keep her eye on the bulletin board and to be first in line for anything that looked promising.

The winter was a severe one and the old house required a great deal of fuel. The Garritys were as messy as ever. The wind broke branches from the trees and they let them lie where they fell. Their endless papers blew over the hedge or landed on it; the dirt-stained snow piled in huge, icy mounds around the garden and a litter of cans, cardboard cartons and a broken-down chair crowned the summit. Mrs. Trowbridge found something to distress her every time she looked out of the windows. And to cap the climax, the Garrity boy came to ask for the loan of their snow shovel and returned it broken.

"I've never felt this way about neighbors before," she cried, "but then, I've never had neighbors like this before!"

"Maybe they'll move," her husband said, from behind his paper. "I've heard that the house is up for sale."

"You have?" Mrs. Trowbridge said eagerly. "Oh dear," her face fell, "even if they moved, which doesn't seem likely, we'd probably get someone worse. I hardly know what to wish for."

"It'll be better in the spring," Mr. Trowbridge said. "Green."

"*You* don't have to look at it all day long, Henry. Green, you say. Their lawn is a disgrace. You can scarcely find the grass for the weeds."

"Weeds are green, too," Kenny put in, his eyes sparkling.

Spring came with a rush that year. One week there was a drab grayness over everything, and bare branches and dispirited lawns, and the next there were daffodils and a haze of leaves and a promise of warmth in the sunshine. Mrs. Trowbridge turned out the house, Mr. Trowbridge began clearing up the garage and hunting for last year's seeds, and Kenny gave Bozo a new collar. Sue found the spring quality in the air a heady one. She felt happy, and hummed under her breath a great deal; she gazed off un-seeingly while her thoughts were elsewhere, and rooted in the overgrown beds for the first sign of violets.

"I know it's silly, they won't be up yet, but I do it every year," she told Beth one day as they came out of Glee Club together.

"I get a yearning to grub in the earth, too, this time of year," Beth confided.

"Do you have a garden?"

"Just a patch . . . the earth is so hard-packed nothing much will grow. And most of the back yard is needed for laundry space and the shed where we keep the car. But we're terribly excited right now. We're going to move!"

"Have you a place?"

"Yes," Beth said. Her voice was vibrant and quick. She turned her face toward Sue and it was lit with the joy she felt. "We've been looking and looking . . . it's so hard, you know, to find a place that we can have. There aren't many houses available. But this just came on the market recently, and Dad snapped it up. Didn't you see us?"

"See you?" Sue echoed, her mind trying to follow. "How do you mean? Why should I?"

"I thought maybe you saw us looking the place over . . . we've only been there once, and we made up our minds right away. We're going to move next door to you. We're going to be your neighbors!"

10.

When Sue got home, her mother met her at the door. Her face looked drawn and she was highly agitated. "I've just had the most dreadful news!" she cried.

Sue's heart gave a lurch. "What happened? Carol— the baby—"

"No, no," her mother said impatiently. She pointed. "That house!"

"What about it?"

"I just heard it's been sold. The Garritys are moving out and Negro people are coming in!"

"Oh," Sue said in relief. "Yes, I know."

"You *know*?" her mother stared at her in horrified surprise. "Do you mean to say you knew this and didn't tell me?"

"I heard it not half an hour ago," Sue said. "From Beth herself. They're so happy."

"Beth . . ." her mother repeated.

"Beth Varley. The girl I've told you about."

"Varley! So that's who it is!" She twisted her hands together in distress. "Oh, this makes it all the worse! I don't know how I shall live through this."

"But why, Mom? Why be so upset?"

"Why? I don't know what's come over you. Don't you realize what this does to the neighborhood? It's bad enough as it is, but now—"

"The Varleys are nice people."

"Do you know the family, too?"

"No," Sue admitted, "but judging by Beth. . . . And anyhow, they couldn't be worse than the Garritys."

"Oh, couldn't they?" her mother's voice became bitterly sarcastic. "I can see you know very little about conditions, Sue."

"But you've never met the Varleys—"

Her mother said sharply, "And I don't intend to. . . . What's more, I don't care how fine the Varleys may be, it's a shame and a pity that the Garritys had to go behind everyone's backs and sell to Negroes. It's a detriment to the neighborhood; property values will go down at once; if

we ever want to sell—and I for one can't sell soon enough
—we'll be the losers. It's the beginning of the end so far
as property values go. But of course the Garritys wouldn't
care about a thing like that. They have no civic pride, no
personal pride."

Susan had a sinking feeling. It was going to be even
worse than she had anticipated. When Beth had told her
the news she had been delighted—for a moment—and had
cried, "Wonderful! I'm so glad, Beth!" But then cold
realization had set in. She was aware of her mother's dislike of the situation, she knew very well how she would
react. It would be hard to convince her that this was no
tragedy—that it might even be a pleasant situation if she
would not be prejudiced against it from the first. For these
were the Varleys, and if her family was at all like Beth
they would be good neighbors and friends. Or *could* be.
But not with this beginning. Her mother's attitude was
one of sharp indignation and dread, and Sue was afraid
that nothing she could say now would help matters
any.

Her father was so much more broadminded. To him
people were people and color didn't matter. She knew that
the Varleys' coming would not disturb him, that he would
be, in his brief intervals at home, as friendly to them as he
would to any other neighbor.

But her mother was another story.

All the way home she had tried to foresee her mother's
arguments and to meet them with arguments of her own.
And, knowing her mother as she did, she knew that they
would be futile, certainly at first. Perhaps in time Laura

Trowbridge's antagonism would die down, she would look the situation in the face and find its best aspect. Only not now. Now she was aghast and angry. Sue saw how she moved about the rooms, with quick, staccato movements, flicking things, lifting them up and setting them down sharply; how she looked out of the window again and again at the Garritys' unsightly lawn, and Susan was sure that in her mind she was comparing this disorder to an even greater one that she felt would follow.

She did not know how to combat her mother's dismay. Perhaps the best thing just now was to say nothing, to do nothing that would upset her. To let events take their course.

Mrs. Trowbridge did not feel that way. When her husband arrived, she barely took time to greet him before she launched into her grievance. He took it silently, Sue noted, but he was an easy-going man—he was not easily roused to anger or to action.

"Well now, Laura, it won't be bad—"

"How can you talk like that, Henry! You know as well as I what will happen to our property. It will deteriorate in value, and we paid enough for it as it was, all things considered. What are you going to do about it?"

"Do?" he echoed. "Why should I do anything? If it was a bona fide sale, it was a sale. It's not *my* house."

"But it's next door to your house," she said swiftly. "Think what it means to the neighborhood—to us, first of all. If it happens once, it can happen again and again, until we're surrounded, and then *our* property will have no value."

"Laura," he said patiently, "there is such a thing as non-discrimination in rentals. You know that. You're being emotional. Sight unseen you're condemning this Negro family who's moving in. When it comes down to it, you didn't like the Garritys, either, and they were white."

"That's beside the point," she replied with spirit. Color rose in her cheeks. "It was a white neighborhood when we moved here—"

"And also a semi-commercial zone," he reminded her.

"I know that! I wouldn't have minded a shop of some kind, or offices. It would still have been a white neighborhood. But if one Negro family moves in, others will; and then where are we?"

Mr. Trowbridge sighed. "The law is the law, Laura. I wish you'd remember that. Why can't you accept it, and make the best of it?"

"Even so," she cried, "the Garritys must know that there's a kind of silent agreement. . . ."

He said drily, "The Garritys aren't the 'silent agreement' kind. If they wanted to sell, I imagine the first party who met their price was all right by them. And anyhow, Laura, I can't see why you're so bothered about this."

"Can't you?" she flashed at him, whisking the centerpiece off the table preparatory to setting it. "Wait and see, Henry. You and Sue seem to have taken leave of your common sense, but I'm not giving up yet. If neither of you will help, I intend to find out what I can about this. I'll not have our prospects ruined without at least a fight!"

Sue had kept still as long as she could. "Mom, you don't know the Varleys!"

"Neither do you," her mother answered. "Except that Beth. You don't know where they live, or how, or what they're like. And I want to tell you this, Susan Trowbridge," she said, putting down a handful of table silver with a ringing sound, "if they move here—which I hope and pray can be averted—I intend to have nothing to do with them, and I don't want you to know them, either!"

Sue's face grew pale. "But, Mom! I *do* know Beth. I like her. She's a school-mate. We're in the Glee Club together."

"You can't avoid seeing her in school or in Glee Club," her mother said. "So be it. But you needn't carry it further. You've gone too far as it is, and *I've* had all I can stand. If you don't realize what you're doing, I do. What's more, they probably chose this place just because their daughter knows you and they think that will help them in the neighborhood. But it won't," she said tensely. "We'll have nothing to do with any of them."

Susan felt as if there were a great lump in her chest. It was hard to breathe. Even discounting the tension of the moment, she knew that it was going to be a difficult period ahead, and she dreaded it. Her own swift joy, that had matched Beth's, was completely gone now, and in its place was a curious, frustrated feeling . . . as if she must do something, but did not know what. As if she must go down a road and the road was barred. How could she act as her mother wished—even commanded—her to act, and yet act as she believed was right? There would be this constant battle between her instinct, her convictions, and her home. For a swift, intense moment she wished that they had never come to Brookhaven and so she would never have had to face this problem. The soft springtime dusk melted into darkness and with it darkness descended on her mind. How did you meet this kind of darkness when it fell?

"Finish setting the table," her mother said brusquely. "I've a thousand things to do, and you're no help, standing there mooning."

The worst of Mrs. Trowbridge's anger wore off in the days that followed, but her stern determination to do something about the situation remained, and she left no stone unturned. Since her husband refused to go, she went to visit various city officials, and came away each time with the same answer . . . there was nothing concrete that could be done. It may have been a flaw in the zoning regulations to begin with, but there it stood—there was no specific phrase forbidding the sale of property in this area to Negroes.

"Then the ordinance should be changed," she said when she came home.

"Even if it were," Mr. Trowbridge reminded her wearily, "it would not affect a sale that has already gone through."

It was with a kind of relief that he took to the road again, and Sue was left to meet her mother's opposition and dismay head on.

But before he went away she had a talk with her father.

"Don't you think it's right—the way I feel?"

"Yes. Don't you?"

"Of course. Only I wish Mom—"

"Your mother will come around in time. She is a woman of strong opinions, and she wants what she believes is best for her family. Right now what has happened is a blow to her. But mark my words, she'll come around. With some people it takes time. And you can't hurry it. It has to come from themselves—not others."

That helped, helped immeasurably. Sue would think about her father's calm words when she was most harassed. In time . . . but when? In time . . . but it was so hard to wait. Particularly when you weren't sure, as he was.

Whatever course she took it was the wrong one. If she said nothing her mother accused her of being insensitive to her distress; but if she tried to present the other side of the question, Mrs. Trowbridge was truly upset and declared that Sue was siding with the Varleys against her own family.

Meanwhile the Garritys moved out, leaving a mass of rubbish behind. "The house was always too big. I never could take care of it," Mrs. Garrity confessed that last day. "I want a little place. For a while we're going to visit around with my relatives and then maybe we'll buy a trailer and go South."

Sue thought irrepressibly, if they can all fit into a trailer it will be the marvel of the age. *Something* will have to give. But she wisely said nothing, and Mrs. Garrity, in a last burst of confidence said:

"It sort of depressed me the way you keep your place so spick and span all the time. But I guess that's the way you are!"

When they were gone, the place looked worse than ever, ill-kempt and deserted, and it was with mixed feelings that the Trowbridges looked forward to the Varleys moving in.

Sue wondered about the place from which they were to come and almost surreptitiously hunted it up one day. It was in a part of town she knew about but had seldom visited, since there was no call to do so. Now she had an active curiosity to spur her on. She memorized the number and walked down to Pine Street on her way home from school. It was an undistinguished street, busy with traffic and teeming with children. The houses were small, set close together, and rather shabby, all of them, with steep wooden steps up to a narrow porch, a door and two windows across the front facade. Little shops with dingy windows and scarred door-frames were set among the houses. A sign hung in front of the Varley house—"Lucius P. Varley, M. D."—and Sue noticed a car in the cinder drive that led, as Beth had said, to the shed in the rear. This house, at least, stood out somewhat from its fellows, because of the way it was kept. But it looked small and hot and unattractive, and she could imagine how the Garrity place would appeal to them, with its larger rooms and big lawn. If the doctor had his offices here too—which must be the case—it would be extremely crowded, she thought.

Early in the week Sue went up to the Bulletin Board with the idea of checking on the Saturday trip to the

Metropolitan and met the notice: "Young woman wanted for recreational assistant at Stafford House for summer months. Part or full time. Call Mr. Wright for appointment."

She stopped short. Stafford House. That was the community recreation center in what some residents of Brookhaven called 'the slum area.' Real estate dealers winced at the phrase, and by common consent, Sue had gathered, most Brookhaven people ignored it because they did not want to admit that there was such an area. She had never been there, only passed it by once or twice when they were out driving.

Recreational assistant. That could mean anything. And was she qualified? Perhaps anyone would qualify, if the salary was too low or they were in desperate need of help. She thought a moment in indecision. Was this the sort of thing she wanted to do for the summer? But what else was there? Nothing very interesting had turned up on the Bulletin Board and the advertisements in the paper were discouragingly emphatic about special training—from running a power sewing machine to being adept on a comptometer. This might be fun . . . and good training as well. It might even pay her for her time, although it omitted that fact and that alone was a little suspicious.

Still, she could at least look into it. Perhaps twenty-five others were also looking into it. She noted Mr. Wright's phone number on a scrap of paper and then, making up her mind suddenly, turned into the phone booth in the corridor and called him at once.

He seemed surprised at such a quick response. "We just

posted the notice this morning," he said. "Can you come down after school for an interview?"

Nothing much to go on, but it seems she *was* the first. She promised to be there at three, and all during morning classes had an odd little feeling of excitement. If she got it, it would be her first real job. *If* she got it. . . .

Mr. Wright was a short, squatty man, somewhere in the middle forties, Sue imagined, with a round pleasant face and sparse hair. He welcomed her cordially, brushing off a mass of papers from a chair where she was to be seated. Sounds of laughter and high shrill children's voices penetrated the thin beaverboard walls and he had to raise his own voice occasionally to be heard.

"I hope you'll excuse the disorder," he said, but she could see that he was not too bothered by it. "We're in something of a turmoil here. The young woman who acts as my secretary has been ill for a week, and things do pile up. I'm executive secretary here, as you perhaps know, and it's up to me to see about getting proper assistance." He gave a short comical sigh. "I'm sure the Board must be glad it doesn't have the responsibility. Help is very difficult to obtain these days."

He seemed to be talking to put her at her ease. He leaned forward, peering at her near-sightedly. "You look rather young—"

"I'll be a senior next year," she said quickly. "And I'm a responsible sort of person."

He nodded. "That we can check on. Do you like children?"

She said quickly, "Very much."

"Know anything about them?"

"I have a brother nine years old," she smiled at him.

"That ought to be fairly comprehensive training!"

"And I've helped at Sunday School—not here, but in Warren where we used to live."

"You haven't lived here long?"

"Only since August," she said, wondering if this would lessen her chances.

"Then I wonder how much you know about Stafford House."

She told what she knew, but it wasn't much.

"Do you know the scope of our work?" he asked. "That we have to care for about a hundred children from a district only three blocks square? And that we're perpetually short-staffed and financially hampered? I say this because it is part of our picture and when you work here you have to come prepared for that and to keep it in mind. We have a teeming center, with never enough people to man it and never enough money to go on. But we all have to accept that—even though we fight against it—and go on from there."

He was watching her as he spoke. "That means, Miss Trowbridge, that you'd be extremely busy all the time you were here, and you'd have to be inventive and ingenious in making things do. And another thing, since our funds are so limited, we can't pay much."

She had felt that was coming. "How much *do* you pay?" she asked forthrightly.

The sum he mentioned was a disappointment to her, but

not too much of one. She hadn't expected much remuneration for her untrained assistance. Whatever she earned would be a boon, when it came to that.

"Would you be able to come full or part time?" he asked.

She countered with another question. "Perhaps you'd like to try me part time and then, if I were satisfactory, you could work me in full time?"

He looked at her in a pleased fashion. "I'm sure I hope you *will* be satisfactory," he said. "Miss Langdon, our director, is staying on, but she will have a vacation period later in the summer, and her assistant, Miss Ducros, had decided to quit as soon as someone to take her place could be found, and our new regular assistant will not come in till fall. I don't suppose—" He broke off, and began again, more decisively, "Could you come part time beginning, say, next week?"

This was a turn she had not expected. He sat watching her and she tried to rearrange her thoughts quickly. It would mean extra money, which would be welcome, but could she carry it along with her school work?

"I could come for two hours in the afternoon," she said at last. "I'm afraid not more than that, if I'm to carry my home work. But when school closes I could come either morning or afternoon and then, later—"

He snapped her up. "At least let us try it that way," he said. "You can find your way in the work, and see how you fit in. I haven't explained about the work, have I? It would be, of course, to help either Miss Langdon or Miss Ducros in whatever way she desired. But more than that, you'd have to keep an eye on the children, amuse them, get them started in games and handwork, tell stories, see that they had their mid-morning lunch or afternoon snack—that sort of thing."

She was relieved. It sounded more or less as if she'd have to take care of half a hundred Kennys. It amused her that Mr. Wright had been so anxious apparently to secure her services that he hadn't even said what the work was to be until she had signified her willingness to undertake it, and then had outlined it only sketchily, as if he did not want to daunt her. But it did not seem difficult at all, and she felt quite confident.

He stood up and she stood, too, ready to depart. "I ought to introduce you to Miss Langdon, but she has her hands more than full," he said, a bit apologetically. "And I ought to show you over the Center . . . but I'm up to my ears in work myself, and you'll soon come to know it, anyhow. I'll telephone your teachers—oh, I see I've not put down their names—"

He scribbled them on a sheet of paper which, she was sure, would soon be lost in the welter on his desk. "And your parents. . . ." For the first time he seemed to look at her sharply. "I suppose your parents are willing for you to undertake this—if your references are satisfactory?"

"They know I intend to work this summer," she said truthfully. "But of course they don't know yet that I have applied for this job. I—I think it will be quite all right."

He said then, "You know, don't you, that nearly all of the children in this neighborhood are Negroes?"

"No," she said, "I didn't. I supposed some of them were—"

"Ninety percent of them are," he said. "Will that make a difference to you?"

"Of course not," she said quickly. She hoped what she was thinking did not show in her face. *She* did not mind . . . but what of her mother?

"Miss Ducros is a Negro as well," Mr. Wright said now, more easily. "Her replacement, the new assistant, is one also. You will meet with her for a while until you are at home here, and she'll try to give you all she can before she leaves—"

Sue said, "I'll be glad to meet her, and to work with her." In a rush she added, "One of the girls I like best— though I still don't know her very well—is Beth Varley."

"Dr. Varley's daughter?"

"Yes."

"A fine family! A splendid man! Well, well, so you know his daughter. In your class at school?"

"Yes, and she's—I mean, they're going to be our neighbors."

"Well, well!" he said again. "I hadn't heard the good doctor was going to move. Now that *will* be fortunate!" For her, or for them, she did not know, but she liked his manner. He shook her hand, and the telephone rang.

"I'll notify you in a day or so," he promised. "I'm sure it will work out. Look around, if you like, on your way through. Make yourself at home." He lifted the phone from its cradle. "Stafford House. . . . A policeman? I'll get one. . . . Yes, yes."

As he hung up a little boy dashed in the office, his eyes rolling. "Mistuh White—kin you git a doctor quick? Ma's fell and broke her leg!"

"Right away, Reggie." He turned to Sue. "I'm surprised we had *that* much time without an interruption or a problem. See you soon, I hope." He waved to her with one hand and picked up the phone again with the other.

11.

To Sue's relief, her mother made no objection to her
taking the Stafford House job when they heard about it.
The fact that it had been okayed by the school, and that it
was one of the Community Chest agencies, seemed to make
it all right, although Mrs. Trowbridge said rather wistfully that she did not see why Sue could not have got work
with one of the other charities and in a more congenial atmosphere. Her father thought it was a good idea for her to

earn some money and gain some experience during the summer, and only Kenny had his doubts.

"Does that mean I've gotta set the table every night?" he demanded, looking up at her through his thick lashes with a scowl.

Sue laughed at him affectionately. "I suppose so. I won't be home in time. But look here, Kenny, if you do, you won't have to dry the dishes. How's that?"

He considered this for a moment and then stuck out his hand solemnly, and they shook on the bargain.

The Varleys moved in on a rainy Saturday, and Sue thought how pleasant it would have been if they could have taken over to the newcomers a dish of 'something hot' or a bunch of flowers, as had been the custom in Warren, to show their neighborliness. As it was, Mrs. Trowbridge seemed to think the end of the world had come—an end which she wanted to ignore; at the same time, she would pause often on her household rounds to peer through the window to see what was taking place.

Kenny was delighted. "They got a boy—like me!" he shouted. "I bet we could—"

"You have your own playmates," his mother said firmly. "You don't need any more."

"But—"

"Don't always argue, Kenny. You heard what I said."

Sue felt sorry for Kenny. In an obscure way she felt sorry for her mother, too. It was a hard time for her to go through, and it was so unnecessary. Things could have been so pleasant! Sue had been curious, too, and liked what she had seen. Mrs. Varley was buxom and compactly built, with a round, jolly face and apparently boundless good humor. The Doctor was a tall man, with lean features and a dignified unhurried air; the sister who, Sue remembered, was studying to be a laboratory technician, was smart-looking and slender, with something of her father's air and build. And Chuckles was just as Beth had said—adorable. She could imagine the mischief he would get into, continually, but he had such an infectious grin, not unlike Kenny's, that she knew he was forgiven and petted and was a happy lad. Together they worked hard and efficiently, setting things to rights—the Trowbridges could hear their excited voices raised in amicable discussion, an occasional burst of laughter, the constant banging of the screen door.

Beth looked happy, but tired, on Monday. "It's wonderful to be in at last," she said. "But there's so much to do—everywhere you look there's something to tackle. We'll just have to take one thing at a time, of course."

Sue wanted desperately to say how happy they were to have them as neighbors, but she could truthfully only speak for herself, and she said nothing, hoping her manner would in some measure make up for her lack of words.

Beth did not seem to notice her silence. "The garden's going to be mine to work in," she said joyfully. "And from the way it looks it will take me years! Perhaps we were foolish to move in so soon, because there's still all the alteration to do."

"Alteration?"

"Yes, Dad's going to have part of the porch made into a waiting room, and do over the little room behind what's to be his office into a dispensary, and then we're to have partitions put up in the attic and make a sort of dormitory out of it . . . but before that's done we'll have all the painting to do; I think we'll do part of that ourselves. To save money, you know."

Sue wondered about the partitions to make a dormitory, but Beth did not enlarge and she didn't want to pry. Maybe it was to be for an overflow of relatives or out-of-town guests.

"It looks as if your summer would be taken care of," she said.

Beth laughed happily. "Oh yes. But I'm taking a part-time job, too, so that I can pay for some singing lessons. I don't want to put any more on Dad than I have to."

"What kind of job, Beth?"

"Housework," Beth said simply. "I'm good at it, and it fits in with the schedule I've set myself—home chores and painting and practice."

Why should she have been surprised that Beth would do housework? It was what you did with a job that mattered, but she herself had never thought of it and, she admitted to herself a little shamefacedly, if she had she probably would have dismissed the idea.

"I have a job, too," she said now, and Beth turned to her.

"You have? What is it?"

Sue told her, and Beth cried, "Why, Sue, that's fine! They do need help down there and you'll get a lot of experience. And have fun, too, I imagine."

"Mr. Wright said he knew your father."

"Oh, yes, Dad's always being called in there, or in the neighborhood. I think he knows most of the people for blocks around. When do you begin?"

"The beginning of the month. Part-time at first, and when school closes, full-time if I'm satisfactory."

"You will be," Beth said comfortably. "What's more, there'll never be a dull moment."

Sue discovered for herself how true that was in her first week at Stafford House. Whenever she approached the building—and the feeling did not wear off, but grew—she was shocked anew at its utter dinginess and shoddiness. Paint peeled from its rotten shingles; the steps needed repair, sagging in the middle from the tread of many feet and broken at the ends. The window frames looked rotten and the panes of glass were ill-fitting, as if they had been replaced too many times. The door was battered and dirty. In the rear, the playground was a bleak area of dust and gravel, with the sandboxes, swings and jungle gyms standing out like landmarks on a desert.

The interior was hardly better. In some ways, as Sue got to know it more intimately, it seemed even worse. For the outside of a building, after all, was what passers-by had to see, but the inside was viewed daily and constantly by the children and the workers. There had been plenty of effort, she could see, to brighten the general effect, but it was a losing battle. What it needed was paint—paint—paint; cheerful curtains, new furniture, re-finished floors. It needed everything, she thought disspiritedly that first day. What was there here to work with? There were games, it was true, and dishes, and a beaten-up piano;

there were low tables and chairs and a phonograph and radio, even a television set. But all of it was either sparse or inadequate or battered almost beyond recognition.

Miss Ducros saw her looking around. "Cheerful place, isn't it?" Her voice was laughing, her meaning unmistakable.

Sue made a little grimace. "Even on a bright day it's depressing. Why, for goodness' sake, why?"

"Because there are too many children for the things we have, and not enough money to buy more or replacements. It's very simple."

Sue said, "Even so, paint would help cover up some of the scars."

"Paint costs money."

"But I thought Stafford House was one of the Community Chest agencies," Sue said, puzzled.

"It is," Miss Ducros said calmly.

"Then why—"

Miss Ducros, busily getting crayons and papers out of a wall cabinet, said, "Did you ever try to get money for something a lot of people thought was unnecessary?"

Sue pondered that, as she helped the recreation assistant set out supplies and as she listened to briefings on some of the children. There wasn't time to do much pondering once they started to come in. The room bulged with them, their voices filled it, their activity seemed to stir up the air as if it were a spoon. At first Sue wondered if she'd ever be able to tell one from another or to remember their names, but very soon she discovered how easy it was, that each was a distinct personality to which a name was attached.

"What you doin' here?" they asked her.

Miss Ducros said, "Miss Trowbridge is going to help me, and when I go she will take my place."

"Don't want her," someone shouted. "Want you! Want you to stay!"

Sue felt deflated, but Miss Ducros said calmly, "They'll get used to you in no time at all. They didn't want me at first, either!"

Their round liquid eyes studied her uncompromisingly, and she returned their gaze with interest. At last they seemed to have decided that she would do, and most of them turned away, to find their own activity, but three or four stood rooted, thumbs in mouths, and lost. Those were the ones to begin with.

"Let's find something to do," she invited them.

When five o'clock came, she could hardly believe that she had been there two hours and her first day was over.

She liked Miss Ducros. She was a small, lively woman with thin features, high-piled hair, and a calm manner. In a few days she managed to give Sue a bird's-eye picture of the background and work at Stafford House, and a thumbnail sketch of each child. "So much depends on knowing them," she said. "But I don't want to tell you everything; that would prejudice you. I just want to tell you enough so that you can understand them and get to know them yourself."

Sue was curious about Stafford House. How had it started? How was it run? And on what? "Air, mostly," Miss Ducros said, with a faint smile. "And good will. And hard work."

Originally it had been a group of stores owned by Mr. Elias Stafford. "He was a nice old man with whiskers," Miss Ducros said. "There's a picture of him over the piano. He owned a lot of real estate in this neighborhood, and when it grew so crowded hereabouts he thought the children should have a central place to play and somewhere to come while their parents worked. So he turned the two stores into one and built a wing on either side and extended the rear. When he died he left the place to the city, with some money. The trouble is, the income from the fund was enough to run the place during his lifetime, but now it has shrunk to about half its size, and it's nowhere near enough. The number of children has increased beyond anything he ever dreamed of, I imagine, and the result—well, you see the result. It's been this way for years, and each year it grows worse."

"But the Chest!" Sue said again.

"The Community Chest allocates a certain sum—just enough, really, to pay the regular workers. For the rest we have to rely on contributions, of which there are never enough, and donations and prayer! It's a nip and tuck affair . . . mostly we wonder how we'll ever come out, but we do. Just barely."

Even in the first week Sue saw what Miss Ducros meant, and what the workers of Stafford House were up against. A gaunt young Negro woman came in. "I've got a chance to get a job at Wheelock's," she said. Wheelock's was the local purse factory. "Jack's left me. I don't know when he'll be back, if ever." She was realistic about it, but underneath, they could tell, was doubt and worry. "I can't leave 'em with my mother—she's got enough on her hands. If you could just take 'em for the day, I'll manage, I guess."

Three more in the bulging rooms. But they took them.

Two pairs of blunt scissors were lost, another came apart. "We'll need more scissors," Sue said.

"We'll have to wait till next month, or buy them ourselves," Miss Ducros said. "There isn't any money just now."

"Could you use some old coffee cans?" Mr. Wright asked, sticking his head in the doorway. "A woman just left a carton full—must be sixteen or more."

"Coffee cans!" Sue cried. But Miss Ducros said, "Of course we can use them. With or without lids?"

"Some of each," Mr. Wright said.

"We can store finger paint in those with lids . . . little toys in those without," Miss Ducros decided, and Sue thought, I'll have to learn to be more inventive if I'm to be worth anything here.

"I don't know how I'll get along without you!" Sue said one day. "I'm going to miss you. Why are you leaving?"

"My fiancé's coming out of the Army, and we're going to be married," she said. Sue, almost unknowingly, looked at her left hand. There was no ring. Miss Ducros saw the glance and smiled. "We're using the ring money to buy furniture for our apartment. Larry has a job in Chicago and we'll move there."

"Will you work, too?" Sue asked.

"There's always work to do among my people," Miss Ducros said.

On pleasant days they supervised the children at play in

the gravelly yard and Miss Ducros took the occasion to tell Sue about various children. "Sarah sucks her thumb because she's shy and wants attention, of course. She's doing it much less since she comes here every day. . . . Reggie's the outspoken kind. He always says what he thinks, and he has a very sunny temper. . . . Ed suspects everybody; the reason is he's always suspected at home. An unhappy child. I wish we could get him out of it."

Sue tried not to, but she soon had her favorites. Eldred who sang as he built imaginary houses and railroad stations and showed them to her with quiet pride; puny little Georgiana, whose thin arms reached around her neck, whose soft voice whispered in her ear, "You tell me 'nother story?" Pam, with two front teeth missing and an enchanting lisp; Gregory who would go off in a corner and solemnly sway in rhythm to whatever music was being played.

There were the serious children and the irrepressible ones; the dull but good-natured ones, the quick, sharp ones. The even-tempered and the little spitfires; the destructive and the creative children.

The interesting thing to Sue, aside from the varying personalities, was that the very smallest ones played together—Negro and white—with complete unconcern and in harmony. They seemed not to know that there was any difference—as, in fact, there wasn't, Sue thought, except in the color of their skins. It was only as they grew older that they began showing concern and forming their own circles. "It's when they begin to hear things at home," Miss Ducros said matter-of-factly, but with a certain sadness, too. "They're all children together until. . . . I keep thinking how wonderful it would be if we could only go on as we begin—just being people together—and how far we have to go until we learn to think that way again."

"Yes," Sue said thoughtfully. "It's all so silly! Why do some of us have to set ourselves apart, as if we were made of different stuff? And what can one *do* about it, anyhow?"

Miss Ducros said, "It takes time, I suppose. And education. But more than that, it has to come from the heart." She gave a small sigh, quickly suppressed. "Only it takes so long!"

> Sue's eyes brightened with a sudden idea. "I have to start the young 'uns on their finger-painting now," she said. "But let's have lunch together and go on talking. There's a lot I'd like to talk about with you."

Miss Ducros paused only a moment. "That's nice of you. We—we might try Mike's, down the street."

"Oh no," Sue cried. "Let's go to Mary Hemming's. Mike's looks like an awful spot—hot and crowded, and it always smells of grease. We could catch a bus to the tea-room, and their service is quick—it's cool there and they have such good salads and desserts."

Miss Ducros was looking in the supply closet for some extra chalks. "I'm afraid," her voice came, a bit muffled, "it'll have to be Mike's, much as I dislike the place."

"But why?" Sue demanded. "We'd really have time—"

Her superior wheeled then. "They wouldn't serve me at the tea-room," she said calmly, "if I went there. Nor you, either, if we were together."

Susan stared at her a moment, while this sank in. "You can't mean that! It's a public restaurant. They'd have to."

"I went with Miss Langdon one day," Miss Ducros said, in an almost dispassionate tone. "There were half a dozen empty tables in front of us, but the hostess said they were all reserved, and besides, we'd have to wait a very long time. . . . We took the hint and left. I don't care to go back. I don't want to go where I have to argue my way in."

Susan felt the blood mounting to her face. "It makes me boil!" she said hotly. "That sort of thing!"

They went to Mike's. Susan ordered blindly; the atmosphere, so thick you could cut it with a knife, took away her appetite. And the food, when it came, left her with no vestige of hunger. Her thoughts were in an angry turmoil. She remembered Schmidt's, and how the High School crowd had usurped the place as their own. She remembered bits she had read and heard . . . Marian Anderson, whose fame had spread over the world and whose voice tore you to bits, being refused hotel rooms and having to lodge with friends. George Washington Carver, that man of genius, asked to address a group of scientists at a hotel, having to come up in the freight elevator and depart by the back door. . . . She looked across at Miss Ducros, small, exquisitely neat, with her keen, intelligent face and lovely eyes. A woman like that refused a seat in a public restaurant. Why? Not because of her mind or her manners. Because of her skin.

Impulsively Sue stretched her hand across the table to Miss Ducros. "I wish—oh, I wish I could do something!"

The Negro woman looked up from her plate. Her smile was calm. "That's how it will come, someday. Because people want it to."

12.

That summer, the Brookhaven Eagle said, was the hottest since the local weather bureau had begun keeping records. Sue was not disposed to argue it.

The mornings, for three weeks on end, were foggy and steamy, the afternoons close and broiling. Rivulets of perspiration ran down Sue's face and neck as she worked, she had to put her hands under cold water repeatedly to be able to separate papers or handle paints; when she told stories—mostly about snow-bound elves and Santa at work in his igloo and princesses lost in a forest hung with icicles —she mopped her forehead and thought longingly of the cold tub awaiting her at home. The rooms of Stafford House seemed to close in on her; the odor of sweat and unwashed little bodies hung ever-present in the still air, and moist imprints of small dirty hands marked every paper.

Sue helped serve cool milk and orange drinks in mid-morning, and the children drank them down and tossed the paper cups in the waste-basket with happy abandon. They played noisily and happily in the graveled back yard, shrieking and sloshing under the spray from the hose, and running till they panted around the yard. "I don't see how they do it!" Sue groaned, trying to find a bit of shade while she supervised them.

Miss Ducros laughed. "They're young," she said. "Heat's partly a state of mind, didn't you know that? And besides, this is heaven for some of them compared to their homes."

Sue had wondered about their homes. She thought she had a fairly good idea of what they were like from passing them each day. But she didn't really know until one of the children reported that Eldred had not come because he was sick.

"Is he very sick?" she asked, thinking of his little pixie face and winning manner.

"I dunno," the child said indifferently.

"I'll go and see at noon," she decided, and in her lunch hour skirted along the hot dusty street, in the deceptive shade of the buildings to Eldred's address. A tall young man, shabbily dressed and with a toothpick dangling from his mouth, lounged in the doorway.

"Is Eldred here?" she asked.

He waited a moment before he answered. His lips barely moved. "Umm, hmm," he said.

"May I see him?"

"Reckon."

"Where is he?"

He seemed too tired to answer. One finger flickered feebly toward the second floor. He slumped still further against the worn doorframe and closed his eyes.

Sue mounted the steps that seemed about to cave in. The walls were almost black from lack of paint, marred with a thousand scratchings and gouged plaster. The floors were uneven and whole strips of wood had been pried loose. The doors were half hung from their hinges; the upper hall was so dark Sue could scarcely find her way. Sue heard a cacophony of voices—a grumbling low voice, children's shrill chatter, a woman's high, sudden laughter. While she hesitated about which door to knock at, a whole family spilled out of one room, bound for the stairs.

"Is this where Eldred lives?" Sue asked quickly.

A stout woman paused. "Land, no," she mumbled. "Next door." She pointed to one half open.

"May I go in?"

"S'pose so," the woman said. "Ain't none of my business."

"Isn't he—your son?"

The woman laughed. "Not mine! Got enough as it is.

Git along with you," she said to her brood, and they clattered down the stairs.

There was no answer to her knock and finally she pushed the door further open and entered. There was no one there. The room was in a state of wild disorder—pots, clothes, a basket with two kittens, and old newspapers all jumbled together on the floor. In a bed with no covers over the mattress lay Eldred, sprawled asleep. She tiptoed over to him, blinking in the gloom, and when she stood above him he suddenly opened his eyes. He recognized her and smiled his sweet smile.

"What's the matter, Eldred?"

"Don't feel good," he said sleepily.

"Shall I get you something? Where's your mother?"

"She workin'."

"And your father, too?"

"Ain't got no father. He daid."

Sue bit her lip in annoyance. She should have remembered. . . . Miss Ducros had told her the family background of so many of the children that it was hard to keep them all apart, but she should have refreshed her mind before she came, or not asked tactless questions. With this spur to her memory she recalled now that Eldred had a sister in a tuberculosis sanitarium, two brothers a little older than he who were temporarily at camp, and a shiftless brother. Could that have been he downstairs? They had all lived together in this room, she realized. At least the shiftless brother could see to getting some food in and clearing up the place a bit. She made ineffectual efforts to get some order out of chaos, and promised Eldred she'd send the doctor, but he demurred at that. He was just hungry, he guessed.

Sue groped her way downstairs, fire in her eye, but the lounger in the doorway was gone. There was no one to ask where he had gone.

She hurried back to Stafford House, aware that she had overstayed her lunch hour, and hunted up Miss Ducros. The young Negro woman listened sympathetically and nodded. "I know," she said. "And that place isn't as bad as some. Eldred's mother tries her best, but things get beyond her, and she's threatened with T. B. herself. She can only work periodically—she shouldn't work at all."

"Do you mean," Sue demanded, "that that place is typical?"

"Yes and no," Miss Ducros said. "It's typical of the kind of house where people live who've let life get beyond them, for one reason or another. Whole families in one or two rooms; too busy or tired to keep things clean and shipshape; conditions getting worse and worse until there's no pride or pleasure in trying to keep their places up."

"Can't they move?"

"Where? Whole districts are closed to them; other areas are too high priced. Even the good Negro districts don't want the poorer element coming in. It's a problem that goes around and around, and yet there's nothing there that some care and paint wouldn't cure—except the overcrowding, of course."

"I had no idea," Sue said slowly, "there were houses like that—"

"A lot of other people haven't, either," Miss Ducros

said, but without rancor. "It's so easy to drive by, or not to come down this way at all."

"But there *are* better neighborhoods—"

"Yes, and I'm in one of them. I have two nice rooms over a little store, and the place is kept spick and span. The trouble is, even in the better neighborhoods, there aren't enough houses or apartments."

One of the 'better neighborhoods,' Susan knew, was where the Varleys had lived. She remembered how drab it had seemed, even so. No wonder they had wanted to get away, to progress upward, to have more space and more ground around them. And if it had been so difficult for them to find a place, how almost impossible it must be for these others who wanted to improve their lot and could find no place that welcomed them.

When Eldred came back he looked wan, but his smile was as sweet as ever. Yet he seemed listless and Sue kept him close to her, and brought little treats for him from home which she gave him when the others weren't looking. She realized that this was foolish and not quite fair; that there were others as deserving and as pathetic as Eldred, that it was only because she had had that intimate glimpse of his home life that she singled him out for her special attention.

After that Sue made a point of going to the homes of the children whenever an occasion offered . . . and there were plenty of occasions. Miss Langdon encouraged her. "After all, you can't really understand a child or his actions until you know where he comes from, and what his home conditions are." And as Mr. Wright had told her, there was never a dull moment at Stafford House. Things were always happening, either to the children or their families.

George's mother broke her leg and had to go to the hospital; it meant finding someone to look after the household in her absence. Henrietta's father was involved in a tavern brawl and lodged in jail, the mother threatened to leave him, the children were in an uproar. Pete's baby sister swallowed a safety pin. The whole Alvarez family was down with food poisoning. The Grantley children got the hives. Little Iva fell off a swing in the playground and cut her forehead, and when she was taken home her mother insisted she was dying, in spite of the child's lusty wails. Bettina got hold of a jar of finger paint and ate it, but nothing untoward happened, except that she had to be given a complete bath, having got as much outside as inside.

Taking children to or from their homes, checking up on their progress, or carrying messages from the staff of the House gave Sue her opportunities. "I wish I could write!" she thought, a hundred times. Stories leaped at her, incidents were gay and tragic . . . colorful always. She said to herself, "At least I'll never sit and moon over what's to be my long theme after this." She would have a thousand things to draw on. But she knew she could never do them justice.

Her mind was crowded with glimpses of other lives—not all unhappy, by any means. There were the happy homes, the carefree ones, the careless households where things went by happenstance but managed to come out all right nevertheless. There were the close-knit families and the loving ones. In spite of poverty there was unity and ambition. There were snatches of song . . . and inviting smells . . . and dancing feet . . . and the excitement of soft voices telling inimitable tales. There was life, in a word. All around her, teeming and turbulent, violent and gaudy, grey and quiet. She felt sometimes as if she were in the center of a whirlpool, looking out, while the waters of this neighborhood swirled about her and she struggled to understand what was tossing around her and touching her on all sides.

It was a stimulating summer, and a challenging one. She forgot the heat for long stretches at a time. At home she luxuriated in her quiet, spacious room, her scented tub and fluffy towels . . . aware now of a new humbleness that these things should be hers, but not someone's else who might be just as deserving. She enlivened the table with stories of her days . . . the funny sayings of the children, the dramatic incidents that were the inevitable result of dealing with a variety of people. She made her family laugh . . . and she touched them, too.

There was never any question now of what should be done with Kenny's outgrown clothes. Sue bundled them to Stafford House, knowing a dozen children who could use them. Kenny said one day, after he'd heard where his striped sport shirt and denim pants had gone,

"He oughta have a plane, too. I got an old one he could have."

His father said, "How old? Does it still fly?"

"Well—"

"You could fix it as good as new, couldn't you, if you tried?"

"Sure," Kenny said eagerly. "All it needs is a coupla new parts. I could buy 'em and fix it up . . . if I had some money."

"How much?"

"Fifty cents maybe?"

"The garage needs sweeping out and the incinerator should be cleaned. That would be worth fifty cents to me."

"Okay," Kenny said quite happily. "I'll do it now . . . then you could give me the fifty cents and I could buy the stuff tomorrow."

Sue beamed at him. He seemed still to be turning something over in his mind. After a moment he went on. "I betcha Chuckles would like to help me. 'Course, he's only eight."

"Chuckles?" Mrs. Trowbridge interrogated.

"The boy next door."

Susan found herself holding her breath. Mrs. Trowbridge lifted her head sharply. "What boy next door? You mean the Varley child?"

"Stuart, yep. They call him Chuckles. He'd like to help, I betcha."

His mother said, "You're to have nothing to do with him; I want you to stay in your own yard. I've told you that before and I don't want to have to repeat it."

"I don't agree, Laura," Mr. Trowbridge said firmly. "Let them play together."

The breath went out of Sue in a long sigh. She knew

that her mother would make no further protest in words, but she knew, too, that inwardly her mother was just as resentful of the Varleys as ever.

How wrong it was! It gave her a queer, guilty feeling. Here she was, working among Negroes and with them, and her family made no objection. Her mother listened sympathetically to stories of the activities at Stafford House, to her first-hand account of conditions on the surrounding streets, to bits of their lives as she retailed them at table. Her mother was willing to send Kenny's clothes to be divided among the children; she had collected some aprons and shirts and shoes from her own and Mr. Trowbridge's belongings. But she would have nothing to do with the family next door.

She could be kind and thoughtful for people she did not know—people who were lumped together in a general vagueness—but the specific and personal, the actual Varley family living beside them, left her cold and bitter. It was hard for Susan to understand it, harder still to live with it day after day.

For the Varleys, to her, were endlessly interesting and she longed to know them better. They seemed to be such a happy, busy family. This whole summer there had been constant activity at the Varley's. Masons repairing the worn cement steps. Carpenters tearing down shingles and replacing them. A man laying a new path to the door. Other carpenters closing in part of the porch. There was hammering and sawing and the sounds of trucking. Mrs. Trowbridge found fault with that, too. And members of the family were busy bringing out trash from the cellar and attic, building huge bonfires, sending things to the Salvation Army, digging in the garden, uprooting old shrubs and replanting them, laying out a vegetable plot, pruning dead wood and raking the drive. Mrs. Trowbridge resented the messiness of the operations, but Mr. Trowbridge kept patiently pointing out that it would look a whole lot better when they got through.

"Yes, perhaps," his wife answered. "If they ever do."

There was a stream of people, too, coming to the house and leaving. Shabbily dressed men and women, some of them; bent and ill, thin and haggard. Old men and young ones, children and babes in arms. "It's as bad as when the Garritys lived there," Mrs. Trowbridge said one day, watching a little group straggle up the walk. "Only now they're all Negroes."

"Naturally," said Mr. Trowbridge, "since they're the doctor's patients."

The whole situation bothered Sue. She could not help feeling that her mother was being rather unfair and, to some extent, stubborn, but there was nothing she could do just now to better matters. She had discovered that saying nothing was the best way of keeping peace . . . but it was an uneasy peace.

She saw Beth in her garden, often early in the morning or in the evening, and would ask her how things were growing.

"Wonderfully!" Beth said, her face lighting up. "Once I give them a chance to grow, they just leap up!"

The sentence stuck in Sue's mind. 'Once you give things a chance to grow. . . .' That was true of people, too.

They needed light and air and the opportunity to expand. And someone to care about them as well.

Once in a while she met Beth coming down her walk when she was on her way to Stafford House and they would go down the street together. Long since Sue had given up caring what others thought about this . . . she didn't care who saw her or what they made of it. She liked Beth; she was her neighbor.

"How are you getting on?" she asked now. "Do you like your place?"

Beth smiled. "Very much. I have a new one, you know."

"No! Since when?"

"Two weeks ago. The first woman had an idea it was wrong to sit down, and she could never seem to remember my name, and nothing suited her, no matter how hard I tried. So I changed. Mrs. Greer is different. I work just as hard, but she's kind. She appreciates little things, and she said I could use her grand piano while she went shopping." Beth's smile broadened. "Of course *that* makes me love her!"

"Of course," Sue grinned back. "I hear you singing, Beth, and your voice sounds lovelier than ever."

"I'm saving my money," Beth said. "Mrs. Greer says she thinks she can get Pavloni to take me . . . he's terribly expensive, but it would be worth having even a few lessons with him. He doesn't take many pupils; I'd be awfully lucky if he would take me on."

"He will when he hears you," Sue said with confidence. She marveled that anyone could withstand the appeal of Beth's rich, full voice, and yet her mother, hearing Beth practice, had professed to be annoyed by the running of scales, the persistent striving for a difficult passage's perfection.

Sue remembered saying, one day, "Oh Mom, doesn't it *do* something to you?"

"Yes, it makes my scalp creep—having to listen to that endless practicing. . . . I never could stand to hear anyone practice," she had added.

And yet of late Sue thought she had caught her mother, on several occasions, standing in a listening attitude as the velvety voice soared and sank in the summer air.

Kenny was unreservedly impressed. "Whee!" he applauded more than once, "she knows how, all right!" And had begun to whistle whatever passage Beth was singing.

"That will do, Kenny." His mother looked annoyed. "Singing *and* whistling is too much."

"But her singing's good!" Kenny protested.

"And your whistling isn't."

That was as close as she had ever come to admitting that Beth had a memorable voice.

Beth was saying now, "I suppose you're getting tired of seeing all that lumber and sand and cement around."

Sue made a murmured protest; *she* didn't mind. She only hoped her mother's displeasure had not wafted across the hedge.

"It won't be awfully long now," Beth went on. "We're trying to get all the outside work done so we can do the painting ourselves inside when it gets colder." She turned impulsively to Sue. "I do think it's going to look so nice! I want you to see it as soon as we're fixed up—I haven't asked you sooner because things *are* in a mess and there's so much to be done."

Sue felt as if a cold finger had been put on her heart. How was she going to meet this? "I'd love to," she managed warmly, but her smile was bleak. She hated having to dissemble, to feel two-faced and, above all, traitorous to her own family. But she thought with sudden resolution, When Beth asks me, I'm going. There's nothing wrong with it, and I wouldn't feel right if I didn't. After all, I have to live with myself.

13.

The high point of the summer at Stafford House was to be a picnic in the park for the younger children. They had been talking about it for weeks and looking forward to it, but Sue didn't know whether or not it would be an unmixed pleasure.

She said as much to Gracie, who had invited her to supper. They sat together on the cool porch, sipping tomato juice. "Don't tell me handling sixty children is going to faze you!" Gracie scoffed.

"If I had eyes on all sides of my head I wouldn't mind. Want to help?"

"No, thank you!" Gracie said with fervor. "I want to enjoy myself in the few remaining days before school opens. Where *did* the summer go?"

"I was too busy to notice," Sue said. "But you should have kept track of it, you weren't doing anything."

"Nasty crack," Gracie said good-naturedly. "Wait till supper. . . . I won't pass the ham twice. . . . I wish," she said, swinging one foot, "I *had* done something. It was an awful bore, just lying around trying to keep cool."

"You could have got your voluntary reading done," Sue said, grinning, and Gracie made a face at her.

"Pete worked on the road gang—you should see his callouses and his bank account!" Gracie said with admiration. "And Mary was a waitress in a summer hotel and met the sweetest boy! And Ginger sold magazine subscriptions and got a lot of Experience, with a capital E, meeting people. And Dave—"

"Yes, I know, he wrote me."

"Oh, he did!" Gracie sat up. "I didn't know he wrote anybody."

"Just a card," Sue had to admit. "But he got a lot on it; said he liked being a camp counsellor—the boys were swell, the food was out of this world, and he'd caught a 13-inch trout. It all seemed to add up to a wonderful vacation."

"I bet he's good as a counsellor," Gracie said. "He's cute, don't you think?"

"No," Sue said positively.

"You *don't*?" Gracie was incredulous. "With that smile and those eyes and that voice—"

"I'd never call him 'cute.' "

"Oh well, you know what I mean! . . . All the girls are keen about him, but he doesn't play favorites—worse luck. I'm surprised he sent you a card." She paused a moment, as if weighing her next words. "You two seemed to get on pretty well together there for a while. Whatever happened?"

Sue considered her answer. She knew perfectly that Gracie realized what was the matter . . . and why David and some of the others whom she most wanted to know had set her apart. She knew, too, that Gracie had angled for this moment, so that she could put the question and could get Sue's response to retail among her crowd. As the year had worn on, she had come to realize that most of her classmates liked her, but they were puzzled by her. She did not entirely fit the pattern they had set for themselves. And while she seemed like them in many ways, she was different in others, and it was this difference they couldn't understand.

"We didn't exactly see eye to eye," Sue said at last. She was afraid the silence had prolonged itself unduly, but Gracie didn't appear to notice.

"Oh heavens, what's that got to do with it? You don't always have to be discussing things, do you? Why don't you just fall in step and act like the rest of us? It's a lot easier."

A little pang shot through Sue and did not entirely disappear even when Gracie continued to smile at her. Why didn't she fall in step? It *would* be a lot easier. You couldn't go through life the way the soldier in the cartoon did—thinking everybody was out of step but you. Sam had told her to forget it; Gracie was telling her to get in step. They were saying the same thing. Be one of us! Come on—we like you, if you don't act queer.

But Sam and Gracie—and all the others like them, who had continued to be friendly with her—were perhaps being that way simply because they were not roused to take sides. They didn't care . . . they just wanted things to go along evenly and smoothly. David—and Judy and Anne—were partisan. They felt strongly; as strongly as she felt. But on the other side. It struck her with sudden force that that was the reason they resented her actions—they felt as strongly as she did. And they all thought they were right!

What was she going to do? How could they ever meet? Or must she go through the next year, too, longing to be one of them, hating her isolation and 'difference' and yet determined to keep her integrity? She felt tired and discouraged at this moment. She was carrying a burden that was too big for her. Gracie was urging her to lay it down and join the crowd. But that wasn't possible, either. While she struggled for a way to reply, so that Gracie would understand, supper was announced and the subject didn't come up again.

The day of the picnic there was a brazen sky. It was hot even before breakfast. When the phone rang, Sue had a wild hope that the picnic had been called off. It was Mr. Wright who announced, in a worried voice, that Miss Ducros was leaving in an hour for Kansas City where her mother was critically ill, and Miss Langdon had a blinding headache. "That leaves you," he said apologetically and as if he didn't have much hope. "I'd go along, but I can't manage it; there must be someone here, particularly now that Miss Langdon's out. I can't disappoint the youngsters . . . some of them were standing outside the door when I arrived. But you can't do it all alone!"

"No," said Sue. It was the kind of day when you really didn't want to do *anything*, much less manage sixty wild-spirited children. But their faces rose before her—Eldred and George and Pam and Sally. She thought rapidly. "If it's all right with you I'll get a couple of people I know to help me out. Would you mind?"

At the moment it was in the lap of the gods whether she *could* persuade anyone to help her; yet she must surely try, for Mr. Wright's voice was one of almost frantic relief. "It would be a God-send! You're a great help to me, Susan. I'll hold the fort till you arrive."

Susan called Gracie. "I'm scarcely out of bed yet!" Gracie moaned.

"You've got to help. I'll do your math problems for a year! Come on, Gracie, you'd love it once you got there."

"I don't believe you for a minute . . . but I *would* like to see what's the great attraction down there that you'll toil and moil all summer for that piddling salary. What do I bring?"

"Yourself. I've got some watermelons and peanuts. A man's going to deliver ice, and Mr. Wright will drive over with the Stafford House supplies and some of the smaller children."

Next she tried Sam. She thought it was a forlorn hope,

but to her joy he said it was too hot to fish and he hadn't anything else to do. "What's my role—snake-charmer, or strong arm?"

"Whatever you like, just so you keep them from falling in the lake or wandering off and getting lost."

"Little Boy Scout, that's me. When do I report?"

"Ten o'clock. I'll get your badge ready! And thanks a million, Sam."

"Don't thank me till you see how many I rescue." And as she was about to hang up he bellowed, "Hey, do I bring my own lunch?"

"No, I'll share my hot-dog with you."

Mrs. Trowbridge packed a lunch for the three of them. Susan protested, but Laura Trowbridge said, busily stowing waxed paper parcels, "Of course you'll want this! Whatever Stafford House provides the children will get away with . . . you can't be eating *their* food."

"What's this?" Susan asked, picking up a small package.

"Band-aids."

"How do we eat those?"

Her mother laughed. "Who knows, you may need them. With a pack of children like that. . . . I've put in some cotton, too, and iodine."

"I hope the iodine doesn't get in the egg salad."

Susan's contribution to the festivities of watermelons and peanuts was stowed in the trunk compartment and Mrs. Trowbridge drove her and Gracie down to the settlement house. "Heavens!" she cried as she drew up and saw the swarming group of children milling around the outside, "*do* you think you can manage?"

"I have your telephone number, madam, if we get

stuck. . . . Thanks, Mom. Come on, Gracie forward into battle!"

Sam arrived on his bike, carrying a knobby looking paper sack, and with some tablespoons sticking out of his pockets. "You brought your lunch—and implements—anyhow?" Sue teased him.

He looked smug. "These are some potatoes that were starting to sprout. Got 'em cheap at the grocer's. And if Mother wonders where her cooking spoons have gone, I'll be able to tell her tonight. We're going to have a potato race, we are . . . or rather, *they* are. I'm just going to supervise."

"A brain!" Sue and Gracie cried in admiration.

It was nearly eleven before they got under way, and the clamor grew by the minute. Sam had gone on ahead with Mr. Wright to prepare the picnic site and stay with the first carload of food till they came. Gracie kept looking around and murmuring under her breath, "What a place! . . . Gosh, what a place!" The children, most of them, had on their best jeans, their well-washed and faded sun-suits, but by now their clothes were mussed, their hands grubby. They clutched at Gracie and milled around her and she drew back against the wall, staring at them with a kind of fascinated horror at first.

The park was not too far away, but it seemed a long distance as they traversed it in the sun. "We should have had a bus!" Gracie muttered, mopping her face.

"A bus costs money," Susan said promptly, and smiled to herself. She sounded like Miss Ducros. By now she had come to think like Miss Ducros. The constant pressure for money had made its dent on her, too. But it was all new to Gracie.

The picnic space was in a shady grove. It felt deliciously cool to them when they reached it. The children flung themselves down on the ground, rolling in the grass, plucking handfuls of it and throwing it over themselves in a kind of ecstasy. Sam had got a fire going in one of the grills and stood clutching himself and pretending to shiver. "Brrrrr," he chattered, making his teeth rattle, "the cold's got into my very bones. Come close, young 'uns, and toast after that long walk in the snow!"

They laughed hilariously, their spirits soaring at once. Sam had a way with children, and Gracie, after a bit, was venturing to make friends with some of the more quiet children. Mr. Wright had left the food, the tub for ice, the pop bottles, the fresh corn. After a while the Negro iceman came, beaming upon them, and deposited the ice in the tub. The children helped range the bottles around it, stooping to lick it with their avid pink tongues. Sam and Susan and Gracie, working busily, undid the hamper, laid out the rows of hot dogs and the roasting forks, split the buns, ranged hamburgers in the wire grills. The children helped shuck the corn and tossed the husks into the fire, shouting as the flames devoured them. Sam was chef, with sixty willing assistants. The girls had their hands full, handing out the finished product, quieting the more vociferous, settling disputes, rescuing fallen hamburgers, shooing away flies.

"Bringing lunch was just a gesture," Susan said, at one point. "We're not going to have *time* to eat."

But at last they did. The watermelon cut and distributed, Susan passed paper plates and told the children there would be a prize for the one who found the most seeds. While they were busy spitting and counting, she and Sam and Gracie downed their own sandwiches.

"Who's that cute little tyke over there?" Sam asked, looking over the circles of boys and girls.

"Eldred," Sue answered, with an almost personal pride. "He's one of my favorites."

"Hi, Eldred," Sam called, "what's that you've got?"

Eldred looked up solemnly and spat three seeds. He reached for the combination of twigs on his lap and held it aloft. "A boat," he said. "I made it. I'm going to sail it by and by."

"Swell. We'll go down to the lake after a while."

Instantly there was a clamor. "We want to sail boats, too! Only we haven't got any! We want boats to sail, too!"

"I'll show you how to make some," Sam said, taking a piece of wrapping paper and beginning to fold it expertly. "Gather round—so you can make your own." While he folded he said in a low voice to Sue, "What about that chap over there—the thin fella with the spindly legs?"

"Pete. He's had polio. He sits and mopes a lot by himself, but he has reason."

"He should have had treatment!" Sam said severely.

"He did; only it was too late to do much good."

"Come over here, Pete," Sam called, without looking up. "You're bigger; you ought to have a bigger boat. . . . I'll start you off and if you watch me you can finish it."

Pete didn't move, and Sam didn't call him again. The

boat began to shape up . . . and all at once Pete, torn between reluctance and eagerness, got up and shuffled over, dragging his one foot. Susan smiled at Sam's triumph, but at Pete's much greater triumph. "You see," Sam was saying, "you do this, and then this—"

"Let me," Pete said. It was almost a command. "I know how. I been watchin'." Sam gave him another sheet of paper, and Pete worked with deft sureness. "Now you go ahead," Sam said, "and make 'em for some of the other guys."

Sue told stories for the smaller children, so that they would rest after eating, and Gracie played cat's cradle with others. After a song-fest, some of the older ones laid out the potatoes under Sam's directions, and they had the race, accompanied by frenzied shrieks and a dozen tumbles. Susan expertly did up the wounds with the band-aids and thought, I must remember to tell Mom about this. While it was under way, Sam took his bike and disappeared; ten minutes later he was back with enough popsickles to go around!

"Sam!" Susan protested, but very pleased. "They'll burst!"

"Not today," he said. "Boy, I never biked so fast in my life; felt a popsickle beginning to trickle and broke all the speed laws."

"Let me pay for them."

"Nothing doing! This is Gracie's and my treat. She gave me the money before I left."

"I don't know," Susan said, out of a full heart, "what I'd have done without you two."

"We don't either," they chorused.

Wilmer, a small wizened boy, came up and plucked at Susan's skirt. "Kin I have the potatoes?" he asked.

"What for, Wilmer?"

"To eat."

"You don't want those old, sprouty things," Sam said. "All battered up from the race."

"Yes, I do," he contradicted. "We kin eat 'em. My ma knows how to make potatoes sixteen kinds of ways."

Sam said carefully, "That's swell. What do you have with the potatoes?"

"Just potatoes," Wilmer said matter-of-factly. "We go down to the Yard and get a hundred pounds. When they're like this we kin have 'em cheap. Ma makes 'em all kinds of ways. They're good."

"Sure, you take them along, then," Sam said. His voice was queer. He looked over at Susan, after Wilmer had run away happily to gather up the scattered potatoes, and she nodded.

"That's not unusual." At the expression on his face she said, "I know how you feel. I felt the same way when I heard it first. And I'm not over it yet."

Gracie said, "Did you bring the rolls?"

Sam roused himself. "Yep, wait a minute." He went over to his bike and took a bag out of the basket. "To feed the ducks, we thought." He held the bag aloft and looked at it oddly. "Only now I don't know—maybe they'd rather eat 'em."

"No," Susan said. She felt old and wise, sad and glad at the same time. "Ordinarily perhaps. But this is a special day. They're really filled up for the time being. It'll be fun to share food with others, if it's only the ducks."

When Mr. Wright came for the youngest ones they were still not willing to go home. It had been a really perfect day. They were mussed and tired, some still splattered with corn grains and watermelon seeds, the whole set off with popsickle stains. But it was a happy little group that trudged back to Stafford House. It would be a day to remember.

Susan said as much to her two companions. "I wouldn't want to do it all the time," Gracie said. "But I sort of envy you, Sue."

And Sam said, sticking out his hand, "Thanks a lot for asking me, Sue. I wouldn't have missed it for all the fish in the river."

14.

Miss Williams surveyed her Problems of American Democracy class with a bright look and Sue studied the new teacher with an appreciative air. She was a small, dynamic woman; copper-colored hair waved back from a smooth brow, her wide-spaced gray eyes were fringed with dark lashes; she wore a becoming shade of lipstick on her well-shaped mouth, and used her hands in effective gestures. "She would look good on a magazine," Sue thought for the tenth time. "She could easily have been a model."

That Miss Williams was a born teacher, however, was evident to the least studious of them. There was enthusiasm in her voice when she talked; she gave every assignment the aspect of a challenge, and discipline was no problem because her pupils had no desire to plague her—she made things too interesting. She was no 'softie,' just the same, and expected more work out of them than most teachers. The proof of her popularity was that she got it.

Susan was as well prepared as any of them this day; she had boned over her lesson, made neat notes, looked things up in the encyclopedia. She hoped Miss Williams would call on her.

But Miss Williams held up their class study book and then laid it aside. "Not everything we learn comes out of a book," she said. "In fact, for us, it is our least concern. I want you to know what's in it, yes, but I want you to know much more besides. With your mind, and with your heart. To know is to understand . . . and to understand is a lifetime job. I can only start you off here. To know yourself, and your family, and your neighbors and your town. Knowing yourself is hardest of all, of course, and comes last. So let's start with the easiest part." Her quick, luminous eyes swept over the group. "Let's just talk today and find out how much we know. Ben, what do you know about Brookhaven?"

Caught off-guard Ben stammered. "Why—uh—I don't —that is, what do you mean?"

Miss Williams smiled disarmingly and leaned across her desk. "I presume we all know that Brookhaven is a town; we know it lies in a cup of hills, and a river flows through it. We know it has a Mayor and a Council, a railroad station, three parks . . . what else?"

The class roused. "Five fire-houses."

"A police court."

"A hospital—"

She snapped that up. "Who runs it? Who contributes to it?"

The answers were forthcoming, and she said at once, "How many of you have been there? As a patient? As a visitor? Do you know the wards?"

Replies began coming more quickly; one reply led to another. She asked about the Library, about the Municipal Building. Had they ever sat in on a court session? How were taxes assessed? What happened to the taxes—how were they apportioned?

"What do you know about the Community Chest?" Miss Williams asked. Looking around the room, she picked Edna.

Edna glibly gave the set-up of the Chest and was able to name most of the agencies it supplied with money. "Now tell me," urged Miss Williams, "what you—personally— know about any one of them."

Ben related some experience at the Y; Edna had helped at the Little Red Door; Bernice knew about the Day Nursery because of her mother's efforts in its behalf; David said his aunt was a visiting nurse and he heard a good deal about the association.

"I know about Stafford House," Sue said. "I worked there this summer."

"Tell us," Miss Williams said.

Sue got to her feet slowly. There was so much to tell, she hardly knew where to begin. The ramshackle House itself; the eager, pathetic, lively children; the gravelly play yard; the battered and inadequate equipment; the devoted women and Mr. Wright who battled endlessly to 'make do.' The homes from which the children came, the cluttered, busy, tragic and happy lives; the milling Center with its phonograph going, somebody tap dancing in a corner, someone else playing an accordion, youngsters bent over finger-painting, the gulped mid-morning lunch, the shabby walls, the shabby furniture, the lack of money—

In the midst of it the bell rang. Miss Williams said, "That's what I mean. We'll go on with this next time. Meanwhile, if any others of you have experiences like that, dig them up and be prepared to talk about them."

In the corridor someone said to Sue, "You sure pulled out all the stops!"

And Judy said, "She's keen! Miss Williams, I mean. But did you really see all that, or were you making it up?"

And David walked part way to next class with her. "You made good use of your summer, I'd say." It warmed her for the rest of the morning.

"I suppose I told it well," Sue admitted to Beth, as they walked home. Beth wasn't in PAD—but Fern and George were, and it struck her that, as she had talked, she hadn't been aware of that fact or tried to change one word because of them. "But now I can't recall what I said. I just know it spilled out, and I wasn't half done when the bell rang."

"That's because it was in your heart," Beth said seriously. "Things come out of you, and really get over to people—like in music—when you feel them."

Beth saw everything from the viewpoint of music; it was her life. Yet it did not make her remote. For the hundredth time Sue wished that her own life was as dedicated as Beth's. She looked almost enviously at the tall girl walking beside her, head high, back straight, and she wondered, for the hundredth time, too, if she would be able to go along as surely as Beth did with so little view of the future. To see only one goal, to bend every effort toward it, and yet not know, really, if you would reach it.

And what was *she* going to do? What was *she* aiming toward? Lately it had seemed to her, just for a flash or two, that she glimpsed something in the distance. But it would fade before she had actually grasped it.

"How's the music going?" Sue asked now. They were both in Glee Club again, but that was not what she meant.

"Oh," Beth said, trying to make her voice casual and not succeeding very well, "it went along fine all summer. Pavloni was wonderful . . . but I couldn't manage many lessons, you know. And now he's gone on a tour . . . he said something about going on when he came back, but that's not so easy. I have to earn the money somehow . . . and we do need a lot of it at home right now. I'll just have to wait, I guess. . . ." Her voice trailed off. "I can always practice, only it's—"

"A long wait," Sue finished. "I know. Money!" she said vehemently. "It seems you can't do anything without it!"

"Oh yes, you can. It's mighty nice to have, and sometimes you absolutely must have it. But not always. Lots of times money hardly counts at all."

"Name three!" Sue challenged her.

But Beth, to Sue's disappointment, didn't take her up. They were approaching their homes, and involuntarily, as if with an inner eagerness, Beth's steps lengthened. She turned impulsively to Sue. "Why don't you come in with me? We're about finished now, and I want you to see everything, before it gets—well, everything looks so *nice* now."

Here was the moment. Why had she been dreading it? Beth was so natural about it, so proud to be asking her, as a friend . . . and she *was* a friend. That was it, Beth was a friend. Sue turned to her. "I can hardly wait to see what you've done!" And that was the truth, too, but not all of it.

The house smelled of paint and varnish and wax and new lumber. Coming in from outside, it seemed dark at first, but Beth pulled on two lamps and called, "Mother, we're home! I've brought Sue!"

A tall, lean young man wearing a slouch hat came down the stairs and brushed by with a muttered greeting.

Sue had only a glimpse of his face, but she wheeled to stare at his retreating back. Something about him struck her as familiar, and she racked her brain. Where had she seen him before? Suddenly it came to her.

"Why—wasn't that Eldred's brother?"

"Yes," Beth answered. "I'm sorry he went out in such a hurry. He doesn't talk much. He's staying with us."

"Staying with you?" Sue repeated, feeling stupid.

"In the dormitory," Beth said. "Now that he'll be out I can show it to you, too."

Mrs. Varley came forward from the kitchen, her broad face creased in a welcoming smile, and wiping her hands on her apron. "I'm making cookies," she explained. "The first batch is just ready to go in the oven, so they'll be ready when you get through. And I imagine Chuckles and Eldred will come in, too; they're playing on the side lot."

"That's funny, we didn't see them," Beth said. "But I suppose we were so busy talking. Anyhow, they'll smell the cookies and come running."

"Is *Eldred* with you? You didn't tell me!" Sue cried. "He's a favorite of mine, you know."

"It's just for the day," Beth said. "So he can play with Chuckles. He's staying with another family since his home was broken up." At Sue's look of inquiry she went on, "His mother had T. B., you know, and she's been sent to a sanitarium. Eldred and his brother Ace are all right still, so Dad arranged to have Eldred boarded and we've taken Ace in with us . . . just for a while. Dad thinks he needs a lot of building up, and Mother's good at that. Besides, Dad wants to help him, if he can. . . . Come along, I'll show you from top to bottom."

While they peered in room after room and Sue commented on things, Beth continued her story. The dormitory proved to be a long room in the attic; the pine boards were not yet painted, but bright red curtains hung at the small windows; there were three beds and bureaus—"they still have to be re-finished," Beth said, "they *do* look pretty battered, we got them second-hand"—and some straight chairs. It was Spartan and simple, but managed to have a welcoming, friendly look.

Sue was fitting things together. "Is this part of your father's work?"

"Dad believes in more than medicine," Beth said earnestly. "He says lots of times medicine is only part of the cure—sometimes it doesn't enter into it at all. He likes to take in people he thinks need building up or helping mentally, and then when he thinks they're ready, send them out to meet the world. Like with Ace. He's so droopy, Dad says, because he needs vitamins and things, but also because he's discouraged, and he's discouraged because he's weak. . . . It's a kind of circle and Dad wants to break it."

"Does he do this often?"

"We've always had somebody or other in the house," Beth said with a smile. "It was pretty crowded sometimes where we were before. This time Dad planned a special place; it's a project dear to his heart. Now we can have three at a time up here . . . and a couple more downstairs if we have to."

Remembering the figure that had slouched in the doorway that day she had gone to hunt up Eldred, remembering the monosyllabic replies and desultory air, and trying to recall just how Ace had acted now, she thought she already saw a difference. He carried himself better; he had a more purposeful air, as if he were going somewhere and not just killing time.

So that was what the dormitory was for—to house people whom the doctor was hoping to rehabilitate! That was one of the reasons, Beth had said, why they had wanted a larger house. Sue cried warmly, "I think that's a simply wonderful thing to do!" Her mental picture of Doctor Varley was taking on depth.

"Oh, it doesn't always work out," Beth said, leading the way to the second floor again. "Lots of times he's disappointed . . . but he always says that if it only worked once it would be worthwhile. This is *my* room. Don't you think those curtains look nice? I just finished hemming them."

"Lovely! I need new curtains. Where did you get the material?"

"Graning's; they were having a sale of mill-ends."

"I'll go down tomorrow. Oh, is this your brother?"

The silver-framed photograph showed a young man in a corporal's uniform, the cap rakishly tilted, the eyes laughing.

"Yes, that's Hank," Beth said, her voice colored with pride. "He sent that last week; he's just been made a corporal."

"He looks like he's lots of fun."

"He and Chuckles are the same type—the world's wonderful and everything's good in it. We miss him a lot."

"Did he want to go to Europe? Was he drafted?"

"Yes, he wanted to go," Beth said, standing still and looking fondly at the photograph. "He volunteered. Hank wants to be a mechanic; he wants to have his own garage or machine shop. He had a good job before he left, but he gave it up because he said—well, that this was the only way he'd get to see other countries and meet other peoples.

When he came back, he said, he could always go on from where he was, but if people around the world didn't get to know each other, there mightn't be any job to come back to. . . . He's due for leave in December."

"Maybe he can be here for Christmas with you."

"That would be something! But we're sending on his boxes just in case he doesn't get it. . . . What was that?" she broke off, as a tinkling sound reached them.

"I don't know. It sounded like something breaking."

"Probably Mother dropped a jar; she's doing preserves, too, I know."

Sue looked at her watch. "Heavens, I've got to fly. I had no idea it was so late. Studying, chores, supper—"

"Well, you can't go without trying the cookies!"

"I don't want to."

The cookies, brown and thin and cinnamony, were delicious. Mrs. Varley said, "I don't know where those boys are. I thought they'd be in before this; the smell generally gets them." She reached for a paper napkin. "Take some along to your little brother; I think he'll like them."

Sue protested, but Mrs. Varley proceeded to make a neat, generous package. "Oh, there's the telephone. I'll answer, Beth."

They could hear her soft voice from the office. "No, Doctor Varley was in but he had to go out on call. . . . I'll tell him as soon as he comes back. . . ." The person at the other end apparently wanted to give full symptoms over the phone, and Sue said,

"Say good-bye to your mother for me, Beth. I won't wait. It was fun—and thanks a lot for these!"

Her mother met her at the door. "Did I see you coming out of the Varley house?"

"Yes, Beth asked me in."

"You know how I feel about that." Her mother's voice was stiff with disapproval.

"I know, but Beth asked me. And it's only neighborly." She hurried to enlarge. "They're going to have such a nice place, Mom. They're working hard, and everything looks so—"

"I don't care to hear any more. Not after what just happened."

"What happened?" Sue asked apprehensively.

"I heard a crash and a tinkle in the dining-room and I rushed in and," she paused dramatically, "the middle window was broken! Half the upper pane out! And there were two boys running like deer. One of them I *know* was the Varley child!"

15.

Of course it was Eldred who was the other child. Sue felt speechless with distress. The fact that the children had run away was a black mark against them and Mrs. Trowbridge was full of dire prophecies about what would happen from now on. The whole happy last half hour was wiped out as Sue tried to combat her mother's anger and wondered what she could do to right matters.

While she stood there, the doorbell rang. Sue darted

ahead of her mother to open it. It was Beth, looking serious and holding a small boy by either hand. "We've come to apologize," she said at once.

Mrs. Trowbridge loomed over Sue's shoulder. "Well?" she inquired coldly.

Beth gave a nudge to each child. "We're sorry," they said in unison.

"I threw the ball," Eldred said.

"But I didn't hit it right," Chuckles took him up.

"We didn't mean to hit your window," Eldred continued.

"We weren't supposed to play on the side lot—ball, that is," Chuckles explained. "It was my fault."

"Mine, too."

"I should have known better," Chuckles insisted, his eyes round, his brow furrowed. "I'm older."

"I threw the ball wrong; I'm not very good at it yet," Eldred offered.

In spite of the situation, Sue had all she could do not to laugh; they were so serious, so determined to shoulder the blame in equal parts. But her mother, who usually was sympathetic to small boys, was not amused.

"That still doesn't pay for my broken window," she said stiffly.

"Oh, you must let us pay for it," Beth urged. "Mother said to tell you so; if you'll get a glazier and let us have the bill—"

But at this Mrs. Trowbridge seemed to take affront. "It's not the money," she said. "We can certainly take care of that ourselves. It's the inconvenience . . . and the annoyance."

"We do apologize," Beth said once more. Sue looked at her mother miserably, and Laura Trowbridge pulled herself together.

"Very well," she said. "I'm sorry it happened, too. Just so it doesn't happen again." She turned then and walked away, and Sue said, in a low voice,

"It was good of you to come right over, Beth."

Beth said, still anxiously, "I'm afraid your mother thinks the boys ran away. They did run . . . but they ran in to tell about it and ask what they should do. Chuckles wants us to use fifty cents he has saved up. . . ."

"Mother wouldn't think of it," Sue said, as gently as she could. "It was just one of those things."

"The boys will be more careful after this."

How pleasant it would have been if, at this point, she could have asked Beth and the young culprits in, and cemented the fracture with a little friendly talk! But her mother was rattling pans in the kitchen and the atmosphere was not conducive to this sort of solution. Beth and the boys took their departure and Sue went back slowly, realizing that the incident had only widened the gap between the neighbors when she had been so hopeful that, in some way, they could come together.

On her way kitchenward she spied the little packet of cookies that she had brought home. She must hide them or dispose of them before Kenny came in. If he saw them he would want them, and, as things were now, Mrs. Trowbridge would not let him have them. Involuntarily Sue sighed. How complicated life could get . . . and for what? It was all so silly. Things were worse off now than they had been before. Would they never straighten out?

Miss Williams, the following week, took up matters where she had left them. The class had almost the sensation that there had been no interruption. It was practically as if they were continuing last week's discussion.

"You were telling us about Stafford House, Sue."

Suddenly Gracie raised her hand. "We saw it, too," she said. "I mean, Sam and I did. We went over to help Sue one day. It was every bit as bad as she said."

"But it's not all bad," Sam protested. "The place does so much good you have to look at it right. Sure they need things . . . but they do a lot with what they have."

"Why *do* they need so much?" Miss Williams said. She knew how to ask questions that drew them out, Sue thought.

To her surprise it was Gracie who answered. "There are just too many kids there for the size of the house," she said with warmth. "They swarm. It's a wonder anybody can work. And they haven't nearly enough material of any kind. I don't see how they function at all. You ought to *see* the place!"

"Well," said Miss Williams conversationally, "why can't we? First-hand knowledge is a necessity if we're to understand any problem. I'll make arrangements for us to go down there next PAD period—that will be Wednesday. After that we can *all* talk with some knowledge, instead of just a few of us."

"Oh boy, oh boy, no class Wednesday!" was the first reaction. But others were more realistic. "Don't fool yourself. We'll have to trot down and back, and keep our eyes open and make notes, and, like as not, come up with something bright on the whole business. Me, I'd rather sit right here in class, even if the chairs *are* hard."

The pessimistic ones were right. The trip to Stafford House, however, was an eye-opener to most of them. Mr. Wright met the group and beamed at Sue. "She was a wonderful help to us all summer," he told Miss Williams, with plenty of the class listening in. "I don't know what we would have done without her."

The children buzzed about her and she recognized many familiar faces, but there were new ones, too. Miss Langdon greeted her warmly, and introduced the new assistant, a sweet-faced young Negro woman who, Sue felt at once, did not have Miss Ducros' firmness of character. Between them the class was shown over Stafford House. The situation was unchanged unless, as Mr. Wright said, with a kind of grim whimsicality, it had grown worse. Sometimes he wondered just how far they could squeeze a penny before it came apart in their hands.

Sue was listening to him with only half an ear. What she wanted to hear were the comments of her classmates. How did this strike them? Could they see, in one brief visit, what she knew to be the true picture at Stafford House? Could they see with their hearts as well as their eyes? What did it seem like to them—drab or inspiring, pitiful or challenging?

It was hard to tell from the snatches she heard. Purposely she stood off and took no part in the discussion raging around her. Some were disbelieving, others were untouched . . . but they, she thought, were the kind whom nothing whatever touched; they lived in a void, their lives as dead-level as their voices. It was all she could do not to 'put in her oar,' as Kenny said. To tell hotly what she thought and felt and knew. But wisely she stayed withdrawn, realizing that her words might at this point only prejudice them against her and Stafford House, too. It was for them, after all, to let the impressions and the facts sink in and form a basis of opinion.

In a way, it almost seemed afterwards as if the entire visit to Stafford House were forgotten. There were so many things going on at High these days—the band practicing, the football season beginning, the new clubs forming, the wheels of the Student Council set in motion. David Grinnell was chosen President as a matter of course. Sue believed that she might have stood a good chance herself of being a representative—except for her activities and her views. She still felt strongly that there should have been a Negro chosen for the Council, but when she broached the subject she was met with a brush-off or incredulity.

"What's the matter—can't you find anybody among *us* you like?"

"I suppose Beth Varley's the only one you can see."

"Beth Varley isn't in our home room," she retorted to that.

"But Fern and George are, and a few others. And what of it? They're nice enough and all that, but what's representative about electing one of them? There are only thirty Negroes in the whole Senior Class—only five in this room."

"There ought to be a Negro on the Council, just the same. He could represent the others in the school."

"There never *has* been one on the Council."

"That doesn't mean times can't change."

"Why change when you're satisfied with the way things are? But then, of course, *you* aren't satisfied. Some people always want to stir things up."

She didn't want to stir things up to be unpleasant, Sue protested. She wanted to be just.

"Who's complaining? *They* aren't. Leave well enough alone."

"What's 'well enough'?" Sue was stung to reply. "Times change, and people should change with them."

"Let's change the subject, then. That'll be *some*thing."

David Grinnell was standing off, taking no part in the interchange. Now he came up to her as she wheeled to leave the room. He sauntered along beside her, one long step to her two.

"Quite a little fighter you are. Do you just *like* to take the opposite side?"

"Oh David, don't be unfair!"

"I'm not unfair. I'm curious. D'you like to fight?"

It was on the tip of her tongue to deny it, vehemently, but something—perhaps his tone—made her stop to consider. She said, quite slowly, "Not really. Hardly ever. But sometimes I have to."

"Even when it makes you unpopular?"

She looked up at him then. "Yes," she said steadily, "even when it makes me unpopular."

"Why?"

"You asked that before one time."

"I know."

"It's—well, it's something inside me. I always felt that way, I guess, but Miss Hamilton put it into words for me. She said if you believed in a thing you had to work for it, and fight for it, whether others did or not. Remember?"

He nodded. "I remember something else she said, too."

It was her turn to be surprised. "You do? What?"

"She said—oh, something about how you could change people by your belief and your work. The old girl was right. You changed *me*."

Sue stopped in her tracks; she felt her mouth must be falling open. Somebody pushed her from behind and, with elaborate excuses, passed her. She was unaware of it until David pulled her to one side of the corridor and kept his arm under her elbow as they walked along.

"Yeah, you. Don't act so surprised. That's what she said could happen, didn't she?"

"Yes, but how? What do you mean?"

It was hard for him to say it; she could tell that by the very casualness of his voice. He kept looking straight ahead.

"I like people who mean what they say. I didn't believe you at first—thought you were just a trouble-maker, or maybe trying to call attention to yourself by not running with the herd. A maverick, sort of. But then—"

He paused so long that she asked, "But then?"

"Well, I got to thinking. I had lots of time to think up at camp, in spite of the small fry I had to look after. Lots of things struck me as wrong—only you'd spotted 'em first. And had the courage to say so. I remembered— There goes the bell."

Sue felt as if she'd been strung on wires, and now had fallen to earth. It seemed as if she had trembled on the brink of something important, something important in her relationship with David. And now it was over before it had really begun.

He turned to her and the old familiar grin was there. He looked relieved to have the bell break in, and yet glad that he had at least got that far. "How about a double split at Schmidt's after prison?"

"Love it!" she said happily. "Meet you outside?"

"Outside here, yes. Continued in our next. 'Bye for now."

He loped off and Sue walked in a daze to her next class.

Somehow the day passed . . . Chemistry and English, European History and Math. And school was over. And there was David, waiting for her. She hadn't quite believed it till she saw him standing on the top steps.

They were part of the stream flowing toward Schmidt's. Yet they walked in a world by themselves. The bright autumn day seemed particularly bright . . . probably because I'm happy, Sue thought. It didn't matter whether David went on with what he had been going to say or not. It was enough that he had said as much as he had. He had acknowledged he liked her because she meant what she said.

He meant what he said, too; that was why this admission was a heady thing. He said she had changed him. . . . Not *him* really, she said to herself judiciously; David was still David, and she didn't want him changed too much. But some of his ideas had been changed because of her.

She wondered whether he'd enlarge on that, and decided not to ask him; it must come from him. Maybe he had said all he intended to say just now.

But he *did* go on. Almost as soon as they were in Schmidt's. He said, looking around the crowded, noisy room, "It sort of began here. Remember?" That was where he'd left off, asking her if she 'remembered'—something.

"What began here?" she asked, so that he could go on.

"Oh, the whole thing. You asking why there weren't any Negroes here and me saying loftily it was because the place belonged to us, and we knew it and they knew it. Boy! Those words came back to me up in the woods. I was a prize goof. So are the others who think that way—only they don't know it yet!"

She spooned happily into her double split, looked up at him encouragingly. Her heart was pounding hard.

"You saw things straight from the beginning. Maybe it was because you were an outsider. We'd been with conditions so long we didn't see 'em."

"Oh, I don't know—" she began. "It was just that I was interested in Beth and that made me think of the others, like Fern and George."

"That's what I mean," he took her up with quiet vehemence. "At least you were interested! You were thinking about the other fellow as a person, too. . . . You know," he leaned forward, his split forgotten, "there were a couple of Negro counsellors at camp. I palled around with them some. I'd never known any Negroes really down here, in spite of going to school with them. Just 'Hi,

George,'—that sort of thing. But up there we were thrown together in our work and I got to know them and like them, and we had some bull sessions after the kids were in bed. We got so we could talk right out at each other—no holds barred."

He looked off into space, way beyond her, as if he were seeing one of those bull sessions now, and hearing the others' voices. "I asked Zack one time what it was that bothered them most and he said, 'Not the big things so much as the little things.' I said, 'What do you mean?' And he said, 'Well, sometimes it isn't nearly so important to you that you'll be able to vote, for instance, as it is to have a chap shake hands with you.' And I said, 'Why, guys shake hands with you,' and he said, 'Yes, but you want them to shake your hand as if they weren't aware of any difference, as if they didn't see a difference or think of one. To shake your hand as if you were a guy just like himself.' "

Sue nodded. "I can understand that. No one likes to feel himself apart, especially when he *knows* there's no difference."

David went on, the words coming easily now. "It sort of set me back on my heels, though. And then I got to thinking." He gave a short laugh. "I told you I did a powerful lot of thinking up there! I thought how *I'd* feel if somebody acted toward me as if he were condescending, sort of . . . being a good sport about it and all that. Not seeing that my mind was as good as his, and my manners, and my actions. It would gall me; it'd gall anybody with spirit.

"And I thought of you. How you'd stuck up for Beth Varley. Not because she was a Negro, but because she had a good voice and was a nice kid herself. That took a lot of character. I—I guess I wouldn't believe at first that a girl had that much. You'd wanted Fern and George invited to the party; you'd thanked them in public. I said to myself, 'Here's a gal who's got a new attention-gimmick.' I couldn't see you any other way there for a long while. But when you stuck to your guns and people began falling off from you and you didn't quit then, either, I sort of doubted my judgment. Only I never thought it through till I got with these fellows and was living with them and talking to them and learning what swell guys they were. That put me straight. And then I realized what *you'd* been doing."

Sue looked down at her hand. It was trembling. This was handsome of David; she was afraid he'd see how much she thought of him, of his doing this. But it was typical of him. She thought, That's what I must have sensed in him from the beginning, why I picked him out as one of the boys I'd most like to know and have like *me*. He had disappointed her more than she would ever dare tell him when he had fallen in with the crowd, but he had changed and he was willing to tell her so. And he said *she* had changed him. The double split swam in a misty haze before her and she felt that she couldn't swallow another mouthful, something was choking her.

Judy and Sam drifted by and stopped. Judy's eyebrows raised, but Sam seemed inclined to make it a foursome.

"Move on," David said equably. "We're busy."

"See you tomorrow, Dave," Judy said meaningfully. "There's something I have to talk over with you."

"Okay, that's tomorrow."

"Let's get going," Sam said humorously. "The guy's barely civil."

Sue laughed and called after them. "Sam's a nice boy," she said to Dave. "I'll never forget how he bucked me up the night I walked out on Miss Haynes, even if he didn't understand what it was all about. And he was simply marvelous at the Stafford House picnic . . . he and Gracie both."

"That's another thing. The way you worked down there this summer."

"Well, heavens, you were a camp counsellor—or wasn't that work?"

He brushed that aside. "You know what I mean. I've been hearing things. . . . And after you talked up in class and we had that visit down there—gosh, that was an eye-opener!"

"It's true, what Miss Williams said, isn't it? You don't understand things just seeing them—you have to feel them."

"This isn't apropos . . . or maybe it is. It sort of ties in with what we've been talking about, at that. And it's what prompted this offer of a double split."

"What, David?"

"What you were saying this morning to that bunch of diehards. While I was standing back listening and sizing you up."

"You mean about having a Negro on the Council?"

"Yes. It makes sense. . . . Only, as Zack made me realize, not just because he or she's a Negro but because he or she is a good person to have."

Sue said excitedly, "That's my point! I didn't put it well—in fact, we didn't get off on the right foot because I was too quick; my temper gets the better of me sometimes. I wanted to point that out. That if we find a girl or boy who's got the qualifications—Negro or white—he or she should be put up. And we shouldn't start out by excluding the Negroes from our list of possibilities."

"It could be done," David said slowly, his eyes half closed. "We could sell them on that bill. It would take time, though, and a lot of work. But I bet we could win some others over to our side, and then—maybe not this year—but next, we'll have gotten them started."

Our side. He had said that. That meant that he placed himself with her, believed as she did, was willing to work with her.

"Oh, David," she cried. "I know we could! No matter how little we accomplished, it would be a beginning!"

He looked directly into her eyes. His own were shining. "Eat up, girl!" he ordered her. "Maybe between the two of us we can move a couple of mountains around here."

16.

Coming home from the football game Sue saw Beth kneeling in her garden, a pile of bulbs beside her. She went to lean over the hedge.

"What are you planting *now*?"

Beth looked up; her face was a little tired and strained and she did not smile as quickly as before, but her smile was friendly.

"Tulips," she said briefly.

"Tulips?" Sue repeated. "But you *had* planted your tulips last week and you said that was the time to put them in. Are these more?"

"They're the same ones," Beth said laconically.

"Are you changing them?"

"They got dug up."

"Oh, dear, how annoying! Who did it? Or was it a what?"

"It was a dog," Beth said, busily, placing a bulb right side up and covering it over expertly.

"The wretch!" Suddenly Sue had a thought. "Oh Beth, for goodness' sake, don't tell me it was Bozo!"

"Yes," Beth said simply, "it was." There was no accusation in her voice, but Sue knew how she must feel to have her work destroyed and all to do over again.

She pushed through the hedge. "I'm just terrible sorry. Bozo must have come untied or else Kenny let him loose. I'll send Kenny over but first of all I'm going to help you get the tulips back in. He ought to do it himself, but I don't know how good he'd be."

"It's all right—" Beth began.

"No, it isn't. It was very careless of him."

"Well, I mean these things happen. I suppose Bozo had a bone buried somewhere hereabouts or maybe he thought this was a good place for a new one."

"He's an unregenerate dog!" Sue exclaimed. "And don't you go making excuses for him." She picked up a bulb. "This looks sort of chewed up. Will that matter? And did he do many like this?"

"Not many," Beth said. "Luckily I had some others.

I'll plant the chewed ones in pots—just in case. Oh, I am looking forward to this bed of tulips in the spring! I never had one before!"

Between them they restored order to the ravaged bed, and Sue went home to find Kenny. Beth had been a darling about the whole thing, and Kenny, when discovered in the basement working on a new plane, readily declared he was the culprit. "It won't happen again, though, honest, Sue! I shouldn't have let him loose. . . . . I thought he was better trained."

"Go on over and tell Beth that," Sue said sternly.

Mrs. Trowbridge was disturbed by the incident. "I'd have given anything not to have this happen!" she cried. "Our window broken, and then their flowers dug up. . . . I don't want things to be on that basis. But I hardly expected anything else. We're just out of luck with our neighbors."

Sue wanted to retort that the Varleys might feel the same way, but refrained. How she wished the situation would ease! It was ridiculous—and sad, too—to have neighbors whom you didn't speak to. She hated the guilty feeling she had every time she spoke to Beth, and it would have been such fun to run in and out of each other's houses as the occasion warranted . . . to be neighborly in the true sense of the word.

The worst of it was that this sort of tension should exist between a Negro family and their own while she was working at school to bring a bettering of the situation there. It made her seem like a hypocrite—someone who talked one way and lived another. And yet, surely, anyone who cared to discover it could know that *she* was not that way . . . that she was even at variance with her mother over this. And that hurt more than anything. To be one way while your mother was another. It would never be right until that was ironed out. And the weeks and months went by . . . and all that happened was something like today to make matters worse.

It helped, however, to know that Kenny was really disturbed over Bozo's and his own dereliction, and he acted handsomely—making apologies to the Varleys, offering to pay for the destroyed bulbs, and leading poor Bozo a considerably restricted life for days on end, taking him around the grounds on a leash and uttering stern 'No's' every time the dog nosed near the hedge.

The other bright spot, and one that nothing could dim, was the almost incredible fact that David was now her friend and ally. More than that, he had already set wheels in motion. He wasn't one to indulge in idle talk or airy promises. When he said he was out to help her move mountains, he supplied a lever of his own, the lever of good action and potent sales talk. He had a strategic mind, too, Sue discovered . . . he liked to reason out opponents' moves and then plan his own to offset them before they could take effect. "Comes of playing a decent game of chess," he told her one day, when she commented on it. "I'd say you ought to take it up, but you seem to function pretty well without it."

Susan was occasionally impatient at how slowly things moved—scarcely at all, she complained. For all their intentions, the status quo was just about the same, and she was afraid that whatever impetus there had been to change it would dwindle away with the passing weeks. But David saw it differently.

"The time will come—" he began.

She looked at him. "That phrase sounds so familiar! We had it today in English comp. . . . I remember now. . . . Gerald Massey said it. 'The time shall come when man to man shall be a friend and brother.' I liked it so! It sounded fine, I thought, and then I said to myself, 'Yes, but when?' "

"It depends on us," he said. "Oh, I don't mean you and me. Not *just* you and me, anyhow. . . . It will come when enough people feel about things the way you do. And the way I'm beginning to feel."

"Yes," she said, "Miss Ducros said almost the same thing. But look at the way things are right here! An impasse if there ever was one. We all agree something should be changed . . . but is it? No. We're going on just the same."

"Listen," David said earnestly. "That's where chess comes in. If you played it you'd realize what a game it is. Don't you know you have to lose some things before you can gain others? You deliberately lose pawns, for instance, so you can make use of a bigger piece. You get the little things out of the way. Once in a while you manage to fool the other side by giving away something that doesn't count . . . but not too often. What I'm getting at is, that we're biding our time. When we see a chance, we'll make our big move. Meanwhile we can lay some groundwork."

"It sounds fine," she scoffed in a friendly fashion. "How long do we keep it up?"

"You wait and see. It works, too."

"Meanwhile—" she suggested.

"Meanwhile we can get in some licks in a quiet fashion . . . let's not belabor our point. Let's just point things out as they come up and sort of lay the foundation for when we want to build."

"Aren't you mixing up your metaphors?"

"Sure," he grinned. "I can't do it on a paper for Miss McNellis, so I'm doing it with you. Nice and relaxing."

"I'm glad you feel I'm relaxing."

"I didn't say *you* were relaxing! Far from it. But you're sort of nice to be with anyhow."

"I thank you," she said with mock solemnity.

"Got to run now. Dad's due for a Community Chest rally, and I've got to do some errands for him beforehand. See you tomorrow."

David was right, no doubt. He got as much done, or more, by being relaxed about it, letting events take their course until he was ready to move. It didn't pay to force matters, and that was too much her inclination.

But having David on her side, and having won over Sam and Gracie to her way of thinking, made a tremendous difference. Others now, whose opinions were never their own but were molded by the actions of their stronger-minded contempories, began to waver, then to look at her again, then to think that, because David and Sam and Gracie were on her side, perhaps they ought to be, too.

In PAD that week Miss Williams made use of the fact

that the Community Chest was having its campaign with-
in the month. The talk about the various agencies and
their needs had been quite detailed when suddenly Gracie
spoke up.

"We're always talking about things," she complained.
"Why can't *we* do something, too?"

Sue looked at her in astonishment. If *she* had said that,
or if David had raised the question, it would have been
in line with her own thought. But that Gracie should bring
it up was an event. . . . Gracie the easy-going, happy-
go-lucky.

The class tittered, but Miss Williams said with interest,
"We can always do something. We have to talk first to
get our thoughts in order. But now perhaps it's time for
action. What do you have in mind?"

"Well—" Gracie seemed to be at a loose end now. "I
don't know exactly. It just struck me that everybody talks
about how this should be done, or that, or what a crying
need there is for something . . . and that's as far as it
gets."

"That's what the Community Chest fund-raising is for,"
someone spoke up severely.

"Yes, but they have always had a terrible time raising
the money they ask for, and they never get enough."

"That's because people have so many demands on their
money."

"Or maybe the workers don't work hard enough pulling it out of them."

"Or maybe," that was David, "people don't realize the
needs they're being asked to fill."

"That's more than likely," Miss Williams said. "So what can we do about it?"

"We don't know about all of them," Sam offered, "but we do know about Stafford House, for instance. We saw it with our own eyes. We could tell people how badly money's needed there. We could make out a good case for them."

"You mean go around *talking* to people?" Gwen Bristow said in horror.

"No . . . why not write them letters?"

"Here?"

They looked, almost as one person, at Miss Williams. "Could we do it here?"

"I think," she said at once, "it would be one of the most effective periods we could have."

It was exciting working it out. Of course they would have to have permission from the Chest officials, "but," said Miss Williams, "if I know them, they will be delighted to have this assistance. Maybe others will take up the idea, too, but whether they do or not, it can be *our* project."

The idea of having something to do, to work for, kindled all of them; even the least enthusiastic members of PAD found this a stimulating prospect. Some protested that they couldn't write letters, but Miss Williams poohpoohed that. "If you saw what we all saw, and if you felt strongly about it, you could tell someone about it, couldn't you? That's all a letter is."

The letters were to be done at home—taking any phase of the Center's work that they wished and talking about it from any angle they preferred. Then they would be read and discussed in class. But it was to be an individual matter.

Mr. Sperling, president of the Community Chest, was 'overpowered,' as he put it, to find that young people would work for one of the Chest agencies like that. He came to see them during PAD period to talk about it. "However," he said, "I'm in an embarrassing position. You are going to put all your energy behind getting money for Stafford House. What about the other agencies? We can't play favorites."

"Other schools," said David, "could write letters about other agencies."

"But Stafford House is *ours*," they told him. "We thought of it first."

When he had gone, Ben said, "Why don't we go into this in a big way? We're only thirty here . . . but if we got the whole Senior class to take part, we'd have a hundred and eighty letters to send out."

"Swell!"

"Yes, but they aren't all in PAD."

He met that, after a moment's thought. "No . . . so we could pick out our best letters—the ones that covered the different aspects best—and let the others copy them under their names. . . . They'd be going to different people, so it would be all right."

"How are we going to get them to do it?" someone inquired.

"Grab them by the neck and stand over 'em while they write," someone else suggested.

"Kindness does it. Maybe we'd better invite 'em to cokes or something."

"Why have to do anything? We're all members of the Senior class, aren't we? All for one, and one for all."

Sue was amazed and delighted. What had started out as a strictly home-room project was now a class undertaking. She thought it remarkable how the idea had caught on. But David took it as a matter of course.

"Why not?" he said. "They don't want to be left out of anything—even if it's work." Then, sobering, he said, "Honestly, though, it does turn out that if you feel strongly about something you can sell it to enough others to make it count. And that's what we did."

The letters, as they came in, were remarkable for their variety. To some the shabbiness of the building made the most appeal; to others it was the lack of equipment; to others, the pathetic play-yard and scanty work materials. Some of the boys, with mathematical minds, broke down the Chest allotments for Stafford House and were horrified that such small sums could cover, however inadequately, the needs of the Center. That was the angle they wanted to present. There wasn't enough money for assistants, for maintenance, for supplies; there was not one penny for emergency funds; nothing, of course, for improvements.

The class was jealous of the names they were given to write to. Some had special friends they wanted on their list; others knew of prominent people whose interest they felt could be aroused if they were properly approached; others believed that residents of Brookhaven who had contributed only desultorily to the Chest were the ones to attack with their appeal. And above all, they felt that they were entitled to a choice of names because it had been their idea . . . an idea which now, under Mr. Sperling's administration, had spread to all the High School and to the upper grades in the secondary schools.

"He knows a good thing when he sees it," David commented.

"Why wouldn't he?" Ben answered. "He's head of Sperling and Bates, one of the biggest advertising agencies in New York."

"Maybe we ought to charge him for our brainstorm."

"Let's just give it to him as our contribution to the Chest campaign."

Sue listened happily. To her the most heart-warming thing was that she had the answer to her doubts of weeks ago. Then she had wondered if the visit to Stafford House had made any impression at all on some of the class. But now she knew it had. They had seen, for all their casual attitude, what she had seen. In spite of their deadpan reaction they must have been touched at what they saw . . . for it was there in their letters.

Sue herself had written several. There were so many things to say she couldn't get them all in any one letter. So she was making drafts of the ones she liked best, and if anyone came up with the objection that he 'didn't know what to say,' she'd just hand one of her spares over to him. It seemed to her this was the least she could do, and it gave her a satisfaction out of all proportion to the extra work it entailed.

The class followed the progress of the Chest campaign with unusual interest. They felt that they had a personal stake in it. How effective would their letters be? Would they have helped in getting the fund 'over the top'?

To their amazement, however, letters began coming in to *them*. At first one or two, then half a dozen or more; as the word spread, they discovered that other sections of the Senior class had been written to as well. A few of the letters congratulated them on their public-spiritedness; some said that they did not wish to have outsiders presuming to indicate to them what they should do with their money. This roused a storm of protest in Sue's group, because they had been so careful not to do that very thing. Some of the letters—to their relief—said that the recipients were grateful to know of conditions at Stafford House —they had very little knowledge of the place or had never been there. And some of the letters were written in an angry tone, denouncing them, their teachers, the public school system in general and the Community Chest officials in particular for allowing young people to seem to favor one agency over another—particularly Stafford House which was almost entirely for Negroes.

They were bewildered and hurt, not a little angry. Miss Williams said, "This shows, better than anything I could have told you, that there are still problems in American democracy." PAD suddenly meant something to them now . . . a distinctly personal something.

"But why?" they demanded. "Why should they feel that way? Stafford House is part of the Chest—it's a center right in this town; it isn't something we dreamed up.

Conditions are just as we said they were—they could have gone and seen for themselves if they didn't believe us. And if it's one of the things the Chest supports, what difference does it make who it's for—Negroes or not?"

Miss Williams said, at the end of the discussion, "If you can keep that attitude, you'll be citizens to be proud of. *I'm* proud of you. Everybody gets an A today. . . . But this isn't the end of it, is it?"

"We should say not!" they practically chorused.

When the Chest fund figures were announced, they knew definitely that it was not the 'end of it.' The overall sum asked for this time had been greater than the year before; the workers had not been able, for all their herculean efforts, to raise the entire amount. Additions to allotments which the Chest had hoped to make were therefore to be curtailed; most of them would get no increases at all. Stafford House would have to get along with the same meager amount it had labored under before.

"Now what?" the class asked. "Something's got to be done."

Mr. Sperling had been warm in his praise of their efforts. If it hadn't been for the letters the various students wrote, he doubted whether the Chest would have come through as well as it had. There had been a drive to raise money for a new hospital wing; there had been an intensive Red Cross campaign; there had been an increase in the tax rate; and there was the general rise in the cost of living. All that affected the amount that people felt they could give.

"Just the same that doesn't help our project any. I

guess," said Sam, speaking for all of them, "it's up to us to supply the dough somehow."

"So now," Ben said in a voice they could all hear, "PAD means Problem About Dough."

They laughed, and Miss Williams with them. "With all you brains here," she said, "I'll sit back and let you work it out. Of course something can be done. Five minutes for some quiet concentrated thinking; then let's see what we come up with."

This was fun, Sue thought; this was exciting. You were confronted with a problem; but it wasn't your problem alone. With all of them working on it together, something would come of it. They would have a solution.

When the discussion period began Dave said, "It seems to me we ought to go at it from the angle of what the place needs most . . . and then whether we can supply it."

"Money?"

"Not necessarily," Sue found herself answering. "Paint, maybe, first of all."

"Paint!" That struck a responsive note. "Paint!" The words spread among them and caught their imaginations, the idea took fire and flamed into a project.

"We could paint the place ourselves!"

"Well, anyhow the inside!"

"Count me out on ceilings—but I'll do baseboards."

"We could have teams—divide up, and each give a couple of hours or so."

"If we each contributed a little money we could get the paint and brushes."

"Wholesale . . . my father has a paint store, and I bet he'd give us a discount."

"We could do it Saturdays, or after school."

Ben groaned. "Anything else after school? I work harder after than in."

"All right then," Dave told him, "you can work at night. . . . But no time and a half for over-time. This is all strictly gratis."

The bell rang before they were through, but even so the working outline was there, the enthusiasm was high, the committees had already been formed . . . one to approach Mr. Wright and the Board at Stafford House; one to investigate kinds of paint and costs; one to schedule the volunteers on the basis of their personal contribution of time.

"We'll make it a Christmas present," Sam yelled above the noise of the class breaking up. "Our Christmas present to Stafford House."

Sue felt warm and happy. This was a wonderful development . . . and the best part of it was that it had grown out of their own desires, not out of any prodding. It was a spontaneous offer. There were many details still to be ironed out. But it would go through, of that she was sure. She turned, gathering up her books, and saw Fern and George coming toward the door from the back of the room. Their faces struck her. They were lit with a kind of incredulous delight. She smiled at them with understanding, for she knew what they were feeling, because she was feeling it herself.

17.

Time! Sue thought despairingly. There just wasn't enough of it. She stood at the back of the auditorium, after finishing her job as usher, and looked out over the sea of heads toward the platform. When you were very young, time stretched endlessly, but as you grew older it shortened and shortened until the hours flew as minutes. You never seemed to get done all the things you wanted to do—or were expected to do, she added wryly to herself. And toward the holiday season it was always worse.

The music ended and she sat down. The rustle in the auditorium subsided but her thoughts went whirling on. Today was one of those days.

Edna whispered, "Did you get your long theme done?"

"Yes, but not my shopping."

Edna said sibilantly, "You must be rich! I haven't any money, so I can't shop. Simple."

Sue grinned. "You can always *make* your gifts."

"How helpful! All I can make are bean-bags. They won't do for aunts and grandmothers."

Mr. Grauert, the principal, came to the lectern. "We've been very fortunate," he said, "more so than most schools in the state, in having a wide variety of prizes to award each year. I need hardly go over them—you older students know them, and the Freshmen will soon become acquainted with them. They offer a stimulus to do your best, a reward for superior work or leadership qualities. I like to think that we at Brookhaven High do not exactly *need* these stimuli, but that they add perhaps an extra incentive. Today I have something very exciting to tell you about. Mrs. Franklin Pierce is giving a sum of money to be awarded to a senior girl each year for ten years on the basis of scholarship. It is to be called the Alberta Hallgarten Prize, in memory of her mother, Alberta Hallgarten, and a committee will be set up to administer it. The sum is to be one thousand dollars."

A low whistle, quickly repressed, was heard somewhere in the hall. There was an almost audible gasp. A thousand dollars! Sue wondered what it would be like to be handed that much money. She had never seen it in a lump sum. If, by some miracle, it could be hers, it would be like a fairy's gift, tiding her over the college years, making it easier for her father, for her family, for herself. Like something dropped from heaven. She thought, My marks so far are more than good, I know that. Of course this is only my second year here . . . maybe that would make a difference and it would have to go to someone who had gone all four.

It was almost as if the announcement had been timed, it jibed so well with her thoughts and the situation at home. Her mother was to have an operation in the spring —not a serious one, but they would want a good surgeon; that would take money. And the furnace boiler had sprung a leak and was beyond repair, the furnace people said. A new boiler had been ordered, and it was expensive. And then, two days ago, Carol and Tim, with little Dena, had come for an unexpected visit.

Little Dena had smiled and gurgled through the days, but Carol and Tim were serious—more serious than Sue had ever seen them. "Carol's had nothing but colds lately," Tim said. His voice was anxious, his brow furrowed. "At first we didn't think too much of it—maybe she'd been overdoing, or maybe the house was in a dampish spot. But when she went to the doctor he said she'd have to go to a drier climate. Her—it's her lungs."

They had been aghast, but Mrs. Trowbridge had said stoutly, "Then that's what you must do, and no two ways about it."

"I can always get work out there—Arizona or New

Mexico, and anyhow it would only be for a while. But money's a little tight. . . ."

"We'll manage that," Mr. Trowbridge said, patting Carol's hand.

"It would only be a loan, sir," Tim said eagerly. "Of course I could get one at the bank——"

"You're not to think of it. Besides, I wouldn't charge what the bank does. And there wouldn't be a time limit on payment, either!"

Carol had been the most cheerful of the lot. "You mustn't worry, all of you. Doctor Fitch said I'd be as right as rain if I caught it *now*. And I've always wanted to see the West!" Suddenly she threw her arms around her father. "You're an old *darling*!" she cried.

"And not so old, either, I'd have you know," he said gruffly, and blew his nose so loudly that Dena let out a startled whimper.

So there it was, Susan was saying to herself. Everything seemed to come at once. They were glad things were no worse, and that they *could* manage, but money was going to be in scarce supply this year.

Money. You needed it so many ways, and always more than you had. Money made the world go round. She remembered, in an irrelevant flash, talking to Beth about it that day. How long ago that seemed! And Beth had disagreed with her. Sue could recall just what she had said, and it was odd that she could hear her voice saying it. 'It's mighty nice to have, and sometimes you absolutely must have it, but not always. Lots of times money hardly counts at all.'

Just the same, even Beth couldn't get around this thing

. . . it would be marvelous to have a thousand dollars to further your plans!

She turned to Edna. "Who's Mrs. Franklin Pierce? And Alberta Hallgarten, for that matter?"

Edna waited till they were out in the corridor. "It just shows you're new here. But I'd have thought even you would have stumbled across some items about Mrs. Pierce!"

"Well, she must be wealthy—"

"Floating in the stuff. The Pierces have that big place outside Brookhaven on the way to Charnleigh. You know, old wall worth a million, wrought iron gates, farmland, woods, lily pool, swimming-pool, badminton courts. It's *the* estate around here."

Sue nodded. "I know. But how come? Did she go to Brookhaven High?"

"Her mother did. She died last year. She was a character out of a book. Wonderful old lace and sapphires as big as chick peas. Rustly silks and high-piled white hair. She was a Brain, too. Used to read logarithm tables for fun, and made up her own crossword puzzles."

Sue laughed. "I'm sorry I missed her."

"She's one of our most illustrious alumnae, I guess. She wrote music criticisms for the symphony orchestra and headed all the charitable organizations in town. Used to go to Maine for the summers and Florida for the winters, so you hardly ever saw her, but everybody knew her—by sight, anyhow—and there were all kinds of stories about her."

"And Mrs. Pierce?"

"Oh, she's nothing like her mother, but she *is* proud of her. Basked in her light, I think. *She* wanted to go to High here, but her mother sent her abroad to learn languages and see the world."

"That's what I would like to do!"

"Well, win the prize and start out!" Edna laughed. "Me, I won't even have to try—I'm so far out of the running. But if you go, you could take me along as a baggage-toter or something, couldn't you?"

"When, as, and if," Susan said with humor.

"I'll start packing, then. 'Bye now."

Joking about it was just one way of covering up your feelings. Edna—and plenty of others—had no intentions of trying to win, but for herself it represented a real possibility, Susan thought without egotism. She knew her marks were near the top. She couldn't think of anyone whose marks were as high as hers except Beth and Lee Paige. *Somebody* had to win—wouldn't it be simply marvelous if it were she? Here was something to dream about . . . and aim toward. But she would not let herself think about it much, she decided; the disappointment, when it came, would be too awful to bear.

The painting project at Stafford House went forward with gratifying speed. "Operation Paint Brush," they called it, and the task forces had a friendly rivalry that worked wonders in the way of accomplishment. It was fun . . . no matter how much work it was. The place began to blossom under their efforts, and the children, coming to peek and remaining to stare, fascinated, saw the rooms change under their eyes. Dingy beaverboard grew pristine; plaster walls sprang to life and color, plywood doors and trim glowed with fresh enamel. The rooms were a tangle of ladders and paint buckets and canvas; one crew tackled the ceilings, another the baseboards and trim, another the floors. The girls cleared out the small furniture and sanded and painted until not even the children could recognize some of their old equipment. Rose-colored walls here; soft green there; canary yellow another place. Contrasting furniture, floors glistening with dark stain. Some of the girls unearthed prints that the family no longer wanted; some of the boys made unpainted frames and waxed them. They bought cheap scrim and hemmed new curtains; they mended toys and covered cushions.

"Now all we need," said Ben with sarcasm, "is a mural or two."

"I'll paint a mural," Fern said quietly. They stared at her and then burst into applause. For they were remembering what clever work she had done last year at the Hop, simulating autumn scenery as glimpsed through the big windows of the barren auditorium.

"Do you mean it?"

"I'd love it," she said. "A whole wall to work on!" And her eyes glittered.

So, in the course of time, one wall of the main room became a vista into another world beyond Stafford House itself . . . castles and trees and green fields and knights in armor riding past.

"If they'd let me," Fern said, putting down her brushes reluctantly, "I'd do a different one in each of the small rooms. And, when they got tired of them, paint them a new one."

"You just mention that to Mr. Wright and I bet he'll buy you the paint himself."

The children were entranced, and Fern glowed with pleasure. They were all invited to the Christmas party at Stafford House, and Mr. Wright, sensing a potent bit of publicity, gave the story to the Eagle. It was written up by a reporter who managed to share his enthusiasm with the public, and he insisted on having a photographer come down and take pictures. The crews had long since finished their work, but they cheerfully set up ladders again and gave a realistic, if sham, demonstration of themselves busily painting and sanding. It was run under a heavy caption and Mr. Wright practically rubbed his hands, anticipating forthcoming contributions.

"One picture is worth ten thousand words," he said.

Ben countered, "Maybe. But people may look at the picture and decide the place has everything and doesn't need any help from them!"

The way Mr. Wright's face fell would have been ludicrous if it hadn't been pathetic. As it turned out, that was the general consensus among the reading public. Why did Stafford House need any special help? It had been completely renovated, the work had been done gratis, the House glowed now with color, the children were very lucky, and they themselves could spend their money elsewhere.

If they could have come down, Sue thought with a kind

of despair, and seen it *before* it was painted; if they could come now and see how awful the exterior looked in contrast; if they could step inside and see the meager equipment that looked even dingier now in its attractive surroundings; if they could see the battered jungle gyms and the scrubby back yard where the children played. . . .

"We can't let it stop here," Sam said. He seemed to speak for all of them. "Gosh, this just makes the whole business worse. What's the use of painting up the place if there isn't enough to go in it? Half the stuff is ready to fall apart . . . and anyhow, they need about twice as much as they have. Maybe—"

"Maybe we could do something in the way of raising the money ourselves," David said. "Yes, but what?"

"Don't ask *me* for money," someone said. "I know how some of those people feel. I just haven't got any. The day after I get my allowance it's a thing of the past."

"Here, too! The cost of living has got me by the throat!"

"We could do something without money," Sue found herself saying slowly. It struck her as odd; her words echoed in her ears. Only the other day she had been bemoaning her own lack of it, thinking how much she needed and wanted it, yet now she was suggesting that it wasn't necessary.

There was a shout of derision, and above their voices Ben could be heard demanding, "Such as what?"

"I don't know yet," she said. "For that matter, I don't know that I'll come up with anything. But if we all thought about it—and if we want to do this, *really*—

we'll get some ideas. And one of them will be the right one."

"On which note," David said, laughing, "the meeting is adjourned. Go home and think, my hearties. Anybody coming up with a workable idea—that doesn't cost money —will be awarded a week's free transportation to school on my bike, and a bag of peanuts . . . shelled."

He walked home with Sue. "Are you sure you don't have an idea all ready to sprout under that brown mop of yours?" he demanded.

"Cross my heart. I wish I had."

They walked in companionable silence a moment. "What'll you give me if *I* come up with one?"

"*Two* bags of peanuts," she said promptly. "Shelled and salted."

"I don't know that it's worth the effort," he said loftily, and they both laughed. Then he added, "If I do answer the sixty-four dollar question, I'll collect on it."

"I wish I could ask you in, Dave," Sue said, when they reached her house, "but I've a thousand things to do."

It pleased her to see that he was disappointed. If he were keen, he'd know that she was, too.

"Cheer up," he said. "Long vac. starts Friday. See you then, I hope."

"Call me up when you get a brain wave."

"Not before?"

She laughed. "Oh definitely before, if you think it's going to take you too long."

Kenny was in the dining-room, his airplane paraphernalia spread out over the entire table. Bits and parts were strewn in apparent disorder around him and a sheet of instructions lay open at his right hand. He barely glanced up at her.

"Where's Mother?"

"Down cellar hunting a box to pack stuff for Carol in."

"Couldn't you have got it for her?"

"I didn't know what size she wanted. Anyhow, I've got to get this done. It's to go in the show at school and then maybe I'll give it to the kids at Stafford House." He knew that would melt her.

"That's nice," she said. "Just get all this cleared up in plenty of time to set the table."

"Oh, sure, sure." Already he was absorbed again. "Join piece X to Y. . . ." he was muttering.

Sue went down to help her mother. Mrs. Trowbridge looked tired and her smile was a little wan. "It's not going to be like other Christmases," she said, blowing dust off her hands and standing in a maze of boxes. "Somehow I can't feel the Christmas spirit this year, with Carol off in the West and the uncertainty hanging over us."

"It'll come right, Mother," Sue said, with an upsurge of feeling. "We have to keep thinking that, because it helps. Carol's young and the doctor said it would be right, and *she's* not depressed."

"I know," her mother said forlornly. She whisked the suspicion of a tear from her cheek. "Just the same, I keep thinking how it was other Christmases . . . how it was last year, for that matter. And how happy we were, and all together."

Sue took one of the cartons purposefully in hand. "Come

on, let's try this one. I have my things all wrapped, but I want to write some silly verses to go with them. And then we'll do it up together . . . and I'll make you a good strong cup of tea."

Her mother said suddenly, putting her hand on Sue's arm, "You're a good child, Sue . . . I think a cup of tea *would* be just right. I've been doing too much today."

"As usual," Sue said fondly.

The gaily wrapped packages, done up in their prettiest papers and flaunting bright ribbons and sprigs of holly, somehow lifted their spirits. What's more, they were fitting nicely into the carton and it would need little padding.

"Oh heavens," Sue cried then, "we almost forgot! Kenny's present for Dena! He'd never forgive us if we didn't put that in." Kenny had made a set of four blocks, each with a letter of Dena's name and a picture of an animal on it painted in bright colors. It was really an achievement. "I'll see if he has them ready."

She went toward the dining-room calling loudly, "Kenny!"

There was no answer. Kenny could lose himself utterly in what he was doing. Sometimes it struck her as admirable, and at other times Kenny used it conveniently to get out of hearing what he suspected might be an unwanted chore.

"Kenny!" she called again, this time from the doorway.

Kenny had risen, startled, and whirled toward her. Instead of answering she saw that his face was contorted and one hand was clawing frenziedly at his shirt collar.

He was making frightening noises, between a wheeze and a cough.

Sue ran to the kitchen. "Mother, Mother, come quick! Kenny's choking!"

Her mother rushed in, sized up the situation at once. "Bend your head, Kenny. Is it your saliva? Did you swallow something?"

Kenny managed a distracted nod. His face was red; he was gasping for breath.

"Help me stand him on end," his mother said. But Kenny resisted their efforts. He was too busy trying to breathe to brook interference.

"Call the doctor," Mrs. Trowbridge ordered. "Ask him to come at once." Thoroughly alarmed now, she attempted to get near Kenny but he fought her off.

"There isn't time," Sue said. Her heart was pounding so hard she could scarcely hear her own voice. Terror rose in her. Kenny's face was purpling; his attempt to pull air into his lungs was horrible to hear.

"Oh dear heaven, what can we do?" Mrs. Trowbridge cried. "Kenny—darling—"

Sue ran out of the room, holding her ears. She thought distractedly of everything she had read . . . the one fact stood out that there was no time to lose. Doctor Marsh lived on the other side of town; by the time she got him— if she could reach him on the phone—Kenny might . . . Kenny might. . . . Where could she turn? What did one do in an emergency like this? If only there were someone—

Doctor Varley!

She ran out of the house as if wings were on her feet. Across the lawn, up the steps. Pounded on the door. Mrs. Varley answered. "Ask the doctor—tell him to come quick—Kenny's choking—I'm afraid—"

What if he weren't in? What if . . . he wouldn't come? But he *was* in. Sue stood panting on the doorstep, and in ten seconds he was with her; his black bag in his hand, his tall figure hurrying with her toward their own house.

"It must have been one of those plastic parts he was working with," Sue said, as they ran. "I suppose he had it in his mouth and I startled him and he swallowed it. . . ."

They were back in the dining room; Kenny's face was purple, almost black; his eyes were starting from his head; the sound was terrifying now; it seemed as if it would tear his small wiry body apart. Mrs. Trowbridge's anguished gaze lit on the doctor, on his kindly, concerned face. "Oh doctor—" she cried. "Save him!"

"Get me a stick of wood—a ruler—anything." He spoke quietly, but urgently.

Sue rushed into the living-room, snatched Kenny's school ruler off her mother's desk. The doctor broke it over his knee into a short and long piece.

"Hold his head," he directed Mrs. Trowbridge. "Hard. Don't let him move—if you can."

Desperation lent her strength. Kenny struggled and tossed, but her firm, anxious hands were like a vise.

"A flashlight," he ordered Sue, not turning his head. He took a forceps from his open bag—Sue remembered, in a kind of irrelevant daze, that he had been opening his bag, in readiness, as they tore across the grass.

"Now—train the light on his mouth," he said. "Stand by."

With incredible deftness he had inserted the broken ruler piece in Kenny's mouth, to one side. The frenzied boy clawed at him; kicked his shins. The doctor did not seem to notice. Sue held the big flashlight close, but off at an angle so as not to interfere with the doctor's movements. She found herself praying, Please, God—please— please— The silent prayer going over and over in her mind and her heart. She could not bear to look at Kenny; his blackened face and popping eyes made him almost unrecognizable.

One of the doctor's long-fingered hands pulled out Kenny's tongue and held it, while the other manipulated the forceps. His intent expression told of the seriousness of his actions, but Sue felt a kind of numbed confidence. He knew what he was doing; if anyone could save Kenny, he could. If only—if only—

It seemed a timeless age before she heard a small grunt of approval, and her eyes flew open. She must have closed them momentarily in the potency of her praying. Caught in the forceps' shining metal end was a small green plastic airplane part. Mrs. Trowbridge let go of Kenny's head. Kenny coughed again and again . . . but normally now. He tried to speak, but his voice was gone. Tears rolled down his cheeks and, miraculously, his dark face was lightening and lightening as she looked at it.

Mrs. Trowbridge sobbed in her relief, her voice trembled and she went around to Doctor Varley and clasped his hands in hers. "God bless you," she said. "I can never thank you. . . ."

Sue thought, You can live ten lives in ten seconds. Now that it was over, she felt weak and ready to cry. She looked at the doctor's lean figure as he straightened up and knew that he, too, had been through an ordeal. It seemed to her that his kind face was swimming in a haze of light. Why, she thought in surprise, I *am* crying!

Doctor Varley smiled happily. It was a pleasant, easy smile. He began putting things back in his bag. "I'm glad I was in, Mrs. Trowbridge," he said courteously. "Every moment counts in a thing like this. But now he'll be all right again—faster than you will."

Kenny croaked almost soundlessly, "I—can't—talk!"

"Don't worry. Your voice is gone for a bit because you rasped your throat coughing. . . . I'm afraid I owe you a new ruler, young man."

18.

Kenny, though entirely recovered in short order, allowed himself to be the petted darling of the household for a week, and the hero of his gang. After all, none of *them* had ever choked on an airplane part and had an emergency operation right in his own home!

Mrs. Varley sent over a bowl of home-made ice cream that first evening, and a wedge of chocolate cake that Kenny pronounced the best he had ever tasted. Chuckles had delivered the gift, announcing solemnly that it was for Kenny, but his mother hoped there would be enough for them all to get a taste. Kenny croaked his thanks and allowed his mother to have a nibble or two. When Mr. Trowbridge came home he had to hear all the details. "Only I'm sorry there's no more cake for you," Kenny said.

His mother was still pale from the ordeal she had gone through. Now that it was over, however, she was able to say to Kenny, "You *know* I've told you, dear, never to put things in your mouth."

Kenny grinned at her. "Well, gosh, then, how would I ever eat?" And they knew that he was definitely himself again.

It was only a few days later that Mrs. Trowbridge called Susan and asked her to take something over to the Varleys. "I was never one to return a plate empty," she said, but Sue knew that this was a thank offering in more ways than one. She peeked beneath the napkin. "Oh, Mom, one of your scrumptious apple pies! And those cinnamon pinwheels! Did you leave some for *us?*"

She crossed to the Varley house with pride. This was more than a thank offering and the return of a plate. It was a first sign of neighborliness, and she hoped with all her heart it marked the beginning of a new relationship.

It still seemed a miracle to her that Kenny had been saved to them by the wonder-working hands and quick thinking of Doctor Varley, and she knew that her mother and father—but her mother particularly, because she had been so much a part of it—would never be able to forget that scarifying few minutes when everything depended on the doctor's skill.

Christmas this year would have a new meaning, however different it might be from other years. There was the worry about Carol, but Carol was only gone from them in distance . . . and Kenny was more than ever theirs. Over and above everything else, that fact shone through and around their days.

She spoke about it to Beth. "You're going to have a special Christmas, too. With your brother home. Have you had any word?"

"No," Beth said, a little frown between her smooth brows. "We can't quite understand it. He was so sure he'd get leave . . . and we've been planning on it. But absolutely nothing has come through."

"Maybe he's going to surprise you. Or maybe he's had a little delay—that happens all the time—and he doesn't want to get your hopes up until he knows for sure."

"Yes," Beth said doubtfully. "But it's too bad. Mother's been baking and brewing for a week, and the house is shining, and we're saving the tree until we hear . . . he might get home in time to decorate it, you know. We all feel as if we're strung on wires, waiting."

Sue nodded sympathetically. "I know. Still, he may just pop in on you some evening, or you may get a phone call and there he'll be, right down at Fort Dix. . . ."

"Christmas is going to revolve around Hank," Beth said. "It's to be *his* Christmas. And we're so anxious for him to see the new house!"

"Think how excited *he* must be!" Sue said. "Merry Christmas, Beth. But I'll see you before that."

Dave called her that evening and asked if he could stop over for a few minutes.

"I'm making popcorn balls," she said. "If you want to help."

"Eat?"

"Wrap."

He gave an exaggerated sigh. "The Christmas spirit certainly hasn't got you yet," he said. "But I'll be over. I'm brimming with it. Maybe I can work on you."

She laughed. "Just so you work on the popcorn balls. I'm way behind."

He was defter than she thought he would be, and together they managed to pile up a respectable number of the sugared and wrapped airy balls, although between him and Kenny Sue complained that she had made popcorn for twice as many balls as there turned out to be.

"I came to talk more than work," he told her almost at once. "Gosh, this kitchen smells goods! Aren't you curious about my big idea?"

"Of course, but I know better than to ask. What is it?"

He burst out laughing. "Girls *are* funny." She shook the popper menacingly over his head and he added hastily, "But nice, too. That is, some of them."

"Go on," she ordered. "Give!"

He grinned up at her. "Well, not to keep you in suspense—"

"And to keep me from dribbling popcorn down your neck—"

"This is it. It came to me in a flash. Not in the bath, either. I was listening to a guy do his stuff on the radio, and it struck me that Gerry Brown could do imitations as good as that. And another guy came on later and whistled . . . and even *I* could run him a close second. So I got to thinking what talent there was around the place."

"Your house, you mean?"

"Nasty crack. School, of course. And why couldn't we put on a variety show of our own? There's nothing new in the idea, but there *is* money in it. Because we have plenty of talent. We'd use only the best. . . . The Rhythmaires, for instance. And Tony Silvester and his accordion. Ben and his magic act . . . it's super."

"Beth Varley—" Susan inserted.

"Oh sure. Beth'll probably be our top number," Dave said promptly. "And Gwen Torbush does a nifty bit of tap dancing. Do you get the drift? And what do you think of it?"

"I think it's swell," she said warmly.

"There are plenty of others; we could go into that later, and weed them out so we had only the best. Then there'd have to be somebody to hold the thing together, act as emcee, sort of."

"Yourself?"

"Have it your own way."

"What would we do for a hall?"

"I thought of that."

"Heavens, you must have been wearing yourself out!"

"Never mind," he chided her, grabbing another hand-ful of corn. "Our church has the parish hall to rent. It's reasonable—something like fifteen dollars, plus lights and janitor service. But sometimes they let it for free, if it's for a charitable purpose they approve of. I bet I could sell them on letting us have it for free, all right!" His eyes shone at the mere prospect.

"And if not—"

"What do you mean, 'not'? You're talking to David Grinnell, the super-salesman."

"We could manage the fifteen dollars," she went on calmly. "Oh, Dave, the High's full of good stuff we could call on. Of course it ought to be coordinated . . . not too much alike, and the program not too long."

"We could sell tickets in the school; kids, parents, aunts and uncles. Maybe we could ring doorbells, too, if we had to."

"How many does the hall hold?"

"Four hundred. Four hundred and twenty if you seat them on the window sills and on the chandelier."

"At fifty cents a head—"

"Yes, I'm good at arithmetic, too. Minus expenses, which shouldn't be much, it would be a nice little sum to hand over to Stafford House."

Sue propped her elbows on the table and gazed at David. "It would cost us hardly anything to put on," she said raptly. "David, I think you're a genius."

"I always like a person who's not given to exaggera-tion. . . . So you approve of my answer to the sixty-four dollar question?"

"You said you were going to collect." She pushed the popcorn bowl toward him. "Take it. Take all of it. I'll even make you some more and a box of fudge to boot."

"Thanks." He stood up. "Got to run along now. I'd rather collect in my own good time."

What was there in his words—or was it his voice?—that made the slow color rise to her cheeks? She stood up, lifting her puzzled eyes to his. "I don't see what you mean—"

"You will," he promised. "Later." He reached in his pocket and brought out a small box, its paper slightly crumpled. "Here, I almost forgot. Merry Christmas, in case I don't see you that day."

"Oh David, thank you," she said happily, holding the small unexpected gift in her hands. "May I open it now?"

"You would anyhow. I know girls. Curious. . . . Well, I'll be toddling. Mom's afraid of ladders and I promised to hang stuff on the top branches of the tree. We'll have a lot of details to go over, but we can iron 'em out during vac. and then when school opens we can wow 'em with our idea."

She was tearing off the paper and opening the little box. On some cotton lay a small silver bird for her charm bracelet. The kitchen door slammed and she ran to it and flung it open again.

"David!" she called. "Thanks a million. It's darling!"

Something floated back to her on the wind, but she couldn't be sure what. It sounded like 'So are you.' But that was silly. Who would have thought David would be so shy about waiting to see how his present was received? And, for that matter, who would have thought that he'd *give* her a present? It was all very surprising. But *very* pleasant.

She dangled the miniature silver bird in the light, watching it happily. Kenny came into the kitchen again. "Is Dave gone? I wanted to ask him— What's that?"

"A milestone," Sue said cryptically.

He frowned. "A milestone? It looks like a bird. It *is* a bird."

Sue hugged him and he squirmed. "A bird can also be a milestone, Kenny."

Kenny stuck out his lower lip. "I don't get it," he said crossly.

It had snowed all afternoon of Christmas Eve, and now at dusk the world outside was a fairyland. Feathers of snow were still drifting down through the violet air; high ridges of snow lay on every branch and twig; the hedges and evergreens were weighted with the soft burden, and the lawns and streets melted into one under their spreading white blanket.

Sue stepped onto the porch to recover the paper where it lay half buried. She shook it free and sniffed the spicy air. Lights began to blossom on the high poles and in the houses. She smiled to herself. This was the way it should look—beautiful and peaceful and studded with light. This was the way you should feel—happy and lighthearted and expectant. It was a lovely world, and waiting for the spiritual re-birth of its King it was particularly lovely. Why couldn't you keep that feeling, that expectancy and warmth, all through the year?

A mail truck made virgin tracks in the new-fallen snow. She saw with surprise that it was stopping in front of their house. She drew her sweater close and waited for the man to get out. He dragged a carton from the rear end and came up the walk. "Package for you, Miss! Sign here. . . . Merry Christmas!"

It was from Carol, bless her heart. How happy her mother would be! She carried it into the house, smelling deliciously of all kinds of commingled good things, and called, "Presents from Carol, Mom! Isn't it wonderful they got here in time?"

Mrs. Trowbridge came hurrying forward. Her face wore a glow of pleasure. "Oh, how nice! Now there's nothing missing—except the dears themselves."

Kenny helped pry open the box. "I hope she sent me a bowie knife and some eagle feathers," he kept muttering. "Let's open 'em, Ma, let's!"

"Not till tonight. You carry them in, Kenny, and put them under the tree. . . . It won't be long now, dear," she consoled him.

There was a note tucked in the top of Mrs. Trowbridge's gift. "It's beautiful here, and I love it. I think maybe when I'm well—and I know I shall be soon—we'll stay on. Then you must come to visit us and see for yourselves. Tim is tanned, I'm growing fat, Dena is a butterball. I'll think of you every minute . . . be sure to blow the little angel on the tree a kiss for me."

Mrs. Trowbridge wiped her eyes. "I shall hate for them to be so far away," she said. "But if they're happy—and well—it's all I shall ask."

"And we kin go out every summer and I kin ride horse-back!"

"Covered with eagle feathers and dripping bowie knives, of course," Sue teased him.

"What's the news, Sue?" her mother asked. "Read me the headlines while I get this meat loaf ready. I don't know where the time has gone—it's nearly six and your father will be in any minute."

Sue spread out the paper, still damp in the folds. Blaring black letters marched across the top of the page. "Air disaster—twenty-nine killed."

"Oh dear, another one!" her mother sighed.

"Plane full of men returning home on leave. Craft crashes on takeoff in Bermuda. Army is investigating cause."

"How dreadful! Was there anyone from Brookhaven or nearby?" Mrs. Trowbridge asked, bustling from sink to stove.

"It gives the list . . . I don't see"— There was a pause as Sue ran down the list of names. "Oh, Mom!"

"What is it? Not anyone we know?"

Sue read, in a strangled voice, "Corporal Henry Varley, Brookhaven . . . nearest of kin, Dr. and Mrs. Lucius P. Varley."

Her mother stood very still, and she and Sue looked at each other. The same thought was in both their minds. How terrible that it must happen at all—how terribly sad that it should be at Christmas, as he was hurrying home to be with his family.

"She has lost her son . . . and I still have my own dear

one," Mrs. Trowbridge said softly. "Because of that good man. . . . Sue—"

"Yes, Mom?"

"I'll wash my hands and slip into a coat. Will you come with me? I want to go over and tell Mrs. Varley . . . tell her . . . I want to give her what comfort I can, as one mother to another."

19.

The Brookhaven High Variety was an unqualified success. It all went off easily and beautifully, and no one who
was not on a committee would have had an inkling of
how much work lay behind that smooth-running perform-
ance. The class as a whole had done such a magnificent
job of ticket-selling that they had been forced to rent the
hall for two successive nights and played to a full house
each time. The church had given them the hall free for

one evening but the class insisted on paying the nominal rental for the second. They had transformed the rather barren-looking parish auditorium into a festive place by the lavish use of colored streamers from the corners to the center of the ceiling, by lamps and posters and cut-outs, and by inspired efforts on the part of the electrical crew with gelatins and shifting lights.

David had had a bright idea to facilitate his job as emcee. He had got some old photographs from Mr. Wright of Stafford House as it was and then he had had Fern do some colored sketches of what they wanted it to look like and what they were raising the money for. These were thrown, with striking contrast, on a sheet let down in front of the curtain, and David let them speak largely for themselves. The difference was so striking—and it was a matter of pride for them to show what their painting efforts had already accomplished—that it made an eloquent plea. Then he showed a picture of the gravelly back yard and the battered old equiment. "This is what we're working for tonight," he said simply, and with that the sheet was whisked upward, the lights went down, and the spot picked up The Rhythmaires.

From then on the program whipped along at a quick gay pace. David stood to one side, in the shadow, and his voice rang out easily as he introduced each new act. He kept the tone light, and he had some nice humor, Sue thought proudly, but when he came to Beth he was serious. "We're proud of Beth Varley," he said. "There's never been a voice to equal hers at Brookhaven High. We think she's going places, and you're privileged to hear her before you have to pay seven-seventy a seat for it."

No one—Sue least of all—had thought that Beth would
be able to go through with it, though she had given her
promise that she would sing. It was such a short time
after her brother's death. Sue had approached her deli-
cately. "We'd all understand," she said. "If it's too much
for you, you must say so."

"Why, no," Beth said slowly. "Singing is like breathing
to me. I can't do without it. And it always gave Hank
pleasure. I'll be thinking of Hank when I sing."

She wore a simple gray dress with a square neckline
and a string of crystal beads that glittered with the rise
and fall of her bosom. She held her hands loosely folded,
tilted back her head and opened her mouth. The glorious
music rolled out in a smooth flow of powerful sound. She
sang "Calm as the Night," and "Songs My Mother Taught
Me." And when the applause died down she said quietly,
"I shall sing 'Requiem'." And she sang the moving "Home
is the sailor from the sea. . . . Here he lies where he
longed to be. . . ."

Sue's breath caught in a sob. It had always been one of
her favorites. She knew why Beth was singing it. It had
been one of Hank's favorites, too. Hank's requiem now.
Sung by his sister in a voice that soared and throbbed in
loving memory of him.

There were unashamed tears in the audience, and they
gave her the tribute of a moment's real silence. But it
wasn't sadness that had caught them in its grip. Beth's
love and her gift of song had raised it above that. It
was sheer beauty, and their own memories, that shook
them.

Sue, standing at the back of the hall, overheard an elderly couple sitting in the last row. "What a voice!" the man sighed.

"Yes," his wife agreed. "Too bad she's a Negro."

"She'll have a tough row to hoe—if she makes it at all," the husband said.

"She probably won't," the woman answered. And it was that that made Sue boil with anger. Why should they talk that way? Why should they set Beth apart, because she was a Negro? Why—but this she had to admit— should the way be harder for a Negro than for anyone else, given the same talent, the same mental equipment?

It was the world that had a long way to go—not just people like Beth. But little by little the steps were being taken. Her eyes sought out her mother, sitting well forward in the hall, with Mrs. Varley beside her. That couldn't have happened a few months ago. But now it was actuality. And if it was because her mother's eyes had been opened, and her heart, then it would happen for others when *their* eyes and hearts were opened.

After the show she sought out her mother. Mrs. Kincaid was bearing down upon them. "A wonderful evening!" she beamed. "Such great talent in you young people!"

Mrs. Trowbridge said, "Mrs. Kincaid, I want you to meet Mrs. Varley, my good neighbor."

The beam dimmed, and the voice cooled. "How do you do," she said quickly. Her eyes roved frantically over the milling throng. "I must run—I want to speak to Mrs. Lawlor before she leaves."

Sue glanced at her mother. Far from being crushed by

the incident, Mrs. Trowbridge seemed amused at Mrs. Kincaid's discomfiture. Her smile was a pitying one. She took Mrs. Varley firmly by the elbow. "Let's get out of this mob," she said. "We can stand near the door while you receive congratulations about Beth. I do wish the doctor could have come! She was simply wonderful!"

Backstage everyone was pounding everyone else on the back. Their voices were high pitched and shrill with excitement, laughter rang constantly. The relief—the success—were heady fare.

"If Gil hasn't absconded with the funds," Dave began.

"Gil is staggering under the weight of fifty centses," Gil spoke up truculently. "It's a wonder some of you guys wouldn't help me."

"How much, Gil, how much?"

"Well," he drew it out to tantalize them, "no auditor's gone over this, and I don't know what the light bill will come to exactly, but I'd say—roughly—"

"Spill it, or take the consequences!" they threatened him.

"I'd say, roughly," he went on deliberately, "we made three hundred and forty-odd dollars."

" 'Ray!" they set up a shout, and Ben, the irrepressible, said, "Nothing 'odd' about *our* dollars."

"Let's have a party!"

"Now!"

"What's open?"

"Schmidt's, of course. Schmidt's is the only place for a celebration."

"Okay, let's get going," Dave spoke up. "The clear-up

crew can finish in the morning. The janitor wants to go home, anyway."

George said diffidently, "Well, I guess I'll run along home."

"Nothing doing," Dave answered firmly. "Everybody's got to be in on this. Where's Fern? Come on, Fern. All set? Have we got enough jalopies?"

Sue put her arm through Beth's. "Maybe you don't feel like it, but it *is* an occasion, and it would mean a lot to me if you'd come."

Beth said, "Of course I'll come." For the first time that evening her smile flashed in the old radiant fashion.

They swept through the hall, bidding the bewildered sexton a hilarious good-night; they swept down the dark walk and into the various cars; they piled out, laughing and talking, into Schmidt's.

"More business?" old Mr. Schmidt groaned. "I was going to close in fifteen minutes."

"No, Schmidtty, no!" they cried. "Pul-lease! We promise not to wreck the place. We're so thirsty! Just eighteen cokes, Schmidtty, and some pretzels and crackers and five vanilla sodas and—"

They clustered at the big round table in the back of the room, drew up extra chairs to enlarge the circle. It all had to be gone over again. The Rhythmaires had certainly got them off to a grand start. . . . George had worked wonders with the switchboard. . . . You could hardly keep your feet still when Tony played. Beth's voice churned 'em up inside . . . on and on.

"Brother, have the poor old Juniors got something to live up to now!"

"They can't, that's all."

"But I bet they'll try to do something like it to raise money. They'll want to take over Stafford House when we quit."

"Yes, but we did it first! They better think up something different. Anyhow, they haven't got the talent the Seniors have!"

Mr. Schmidt, bearing a huge tray of drinks and eats, surveyed the animated crowd benevolently. His eyes went shrewdly around the circle, taking them all in, one by one.

"It was a big success?"

"What does it sound like?" they demanded humorously. "You should have been there, Schmidtty."

"How can I be two places at once?"

"We made a lot of money and had a good time."

"It's always a good time when you work together," he said.

They raised their glasses. "Here's to us! All of us!" Dave proposed, and they turned to each other and drank.

"This," said Mr. Schmidt, "I like to see. Maybe now I don't close till eleven-fifteen."

Sue thought about it often afterwards. It was the beginning, and it had come about naturally, as a result of their elation at putting on a successful show together.

"But it mustn't be just for this once," Sue said anxiously.

"It won't. You watch," Dave said with confidence.

And he was right. Word spread, first through the Senior class, then seeping downward through the others, that Schmidt's wasn't 'exclusive' any more. There were a few who didn't like it and tried to set up another 'exclusive' at Joe's Shop, but it didn't work out. They missed the fun of being part of the crowd . . . and the crowd was going to Schmidt's. The leaders had decreed it, and the others followed suit. There would always be a few malcontents, Sue realized, but it surprised her how few there were, after all. The barrier was down, and once it was down no one seemed to think much about it. That was the most surprising thing of all.

Beth was practicing when Sue stopped for her on her way to school. She was still humming as she came to the door.

"You have the poor birds all confused," Sue said. "They're bursting their throats trying to keep up with you, but they can't find the tree you're in."

Beth laughed. "You're no critic—you're just a friend."

"And I don't like that 'just,' " Sue teased her. "Don't you know that line about 'my best friend and severest critic'?"

"You *are* my best friend," Beth said simply. She gave Sue's arm a companionable squeeze. "Come out and see my tulips."

"We'll be late."

"We'll run. You must see them. . . . The very first ones. Somehow the first ones are always best . . . they look so brave and cocky."

The row of scarlet tulips marched in a flaming line down the garden path. Beth's face lit as she looked at them.

"They make me think of Hank," Beth said, bending

over them. "Gay. And like soldiers. Hank would have loved them. He loved everything bright and cheerful." She broke one off short and wove the stem through the buttonholes of Sue's jacket. "I'm going to cut some when I come home and put them by his picture. I wish—oh, I wish he could have seen us in this house, and how happy we are."

"You *are* happy here?" Sue pressed. The answer was important to her.

"Yes," Beth answered, looking straight at her. "It's so good to have neighbors like you. No one else has come," she said simply, "but Mother doesn't mind. She said we're rich to have one good set of neighbors."

Sue thought humbly, And we might almost not have been neighbors at all, in the true sense. It was an accident —and a miracle—that had brought them together. How long would it take others to realize what they were missing? But she dared not censure those others. It had happened in her own family.

How grateful she was that the breach with her mother had been closed! To have her antagonistic and un-understanding had been hardest of all. But it had worked out . . . because it was a matter of feeling with your heart, not just thinking with your mind. When your heart and your mind were agreed, the difficulties melted away and you saw things in their true light. Things, she said to herself, and people. You didn't just see people as figures and moving shapes, different from yourself. You saw them as living, breathing creatures *like* yourself.

She came back from the distance her thoughts had

taken her and heard Beth's words still echoing in the air.

"I'm glad," Sue said. "*We* think we're the lucky ones. . . . How's the dormitory working out?"

"Just as Dad hoped it would. You know about Ace, of course. He loves his job out West; he writes every once in a while. We've had a couple of disappointments, of course, but that was to be expected. The dorm's full now. . . . I guess it will always be full as long as Dad sees a need for it."

Dave met them at the school steps. "Hurry up, slow-pokes!" And when they came abreast, "Sue, I want a word with you."

"It sounds ominous," Beth laughed, as she moved off.

"What's up?" Sue asked, letting him take her books.

"Big things afoot. Greg Folsome called up last night; he's going to resign from the Council. His dad has a job in Schenectady and they're moving right away. He'll submit it at the meeting this afternoon."

"What a shame! He's good."

"Yes, we'll miss him. But here's the chance we've been waiting for."

Sue looked at him, comprehension dawning. "You mean—"

He nodded. "I do. I'm sorry Greg's going and all that, but I couldn't ask for a better chance. It's up to me to appoint someone to take his place. And I'm going to appoint George."

"Oh, Dave! Let me know what happens."

"See you tonight?"

"Yes. I can hardly wait to hear."

"Hey, that's not the only reason, I hope!"

"There goes the bell," she answered obliquely. But she looked up at him and smiled.

She felt on tenterhooks all day. Why shouldn't it go through, she asked herself. Dave would put it across. Yet it mustn't be that—just 'put across,' railroaded through, forced down their necks. That wouldn't mean anything.

Dave dropped by before supper. "I just wanted to satisfy your curiosity," he said. "This doesn't count as part of our date. . . . The secretary read Greg's letter and we accepted it with regret and so forth and so forth, and then I gave my little spiel. I told them there was no use wasting any time, we had a lot of stuff on the agenda and we needed a full and functioning Council, so I was appointing George Bellowes to fill out Greg's unexpired term. I said there was, of course, no vote needed, but I'd appreciate an expression of opinion because we were supposed to work closely together and should be a coordinated team. I didn't play up George. . . . I wanted to see what *they* would say.

"And at first there was a sort of stunned silence, and then a couple of feeble squawks from Judy. But Sam leaped up and said, 'Who could be better? We know what a swell job he did with tickets and lighting on two of our biggest projects; he stands high in his studies, he has a nice personality . . . altogether I think he's a swell fellow.' I wished I could have slapped Sam on the back then and there. But that started it. Once the ice was broken—and by a guy like Sam—it turned into a sort of press party for George. Judy said, 'Well, all we can do is try him . . . though I hope this doesn't spread.' And she got jumped on."

He stretched his arms above his head. "It did me good to hear 'em. I kept thinking of you, wishing *you* could have heard them. . . . I don't know how it'll work out, but why shouldn't it? George has the business sense of a man, and he's likable. If *he* goes over, maybe next year when they start campaigning there'll be a chance for some others. Anyhow—"

Sue said warmly, "Anyhow we've begun it. We've set a precedent. Somebody had to do it, and I'm glad it was our class. I'm glad it was *you*, Dave," she said softly.

"No, it was you," he said seriously.

20.

Sue read the little note over and over, although she knew it by heart. "Will you please meet with the Alberta Hallgarten Prize committee on May seventeenth at three-thirty o'clock in Room 212?" It was signed by Louise Griscom, Chairman.

It seemed incredible. It could mean only one thing, of course. She was to be notified that she was being awarded the prize. One thousand dollars. Was she dreaming? How *could* she be the winner? If I had a pin I'd stick it in me, she thought happily. Working like a beaver all year had paid off. Her average must have been the highest, in spite of that lowish point in History right after the holidays. Oh, what a glorious future could lie ahead! She knew what she wanted to do. It was gratifying to have your mind made up, your course set. Her desires had crystallized during the year, though perhaps, she thought, it had been that summer's work at Stafford House that had really set her off.

She would go to college—Smith, if it wasn't too late, or Wellesley—and major in social studies. She was going to work with people, young people, whenever she got the chance. She liked it; she knew she could make a success of it, a really worthwhile success if she had more knowledge and training and background for her work. There were any number of places crying out for the sort of person she felt she could be. Getting the prize was going to start her off free and clear. She wouldn't need aid from her family—not much, that is, for once at college she knew she could find things to do that would help along with expenses.

Bless this committee, bless Mrs. Franklin Pierce, bless everybody. She could scarcely keep her mind on her work, waiting for three-thirty to come. She was eager to see the rest of the committee; she had no idea who they were. It's just as well I wore my shantung dress, she thought. I must have had a hunch. I do want to present a nice appearance. And I'll rush to the girls' room and do over my hair and put on some powder before I go up. I wish my heart wouldn't bang so hard. And my hands are positively clammy.

One thousand dollars. Tops in her class. Who said it didn't pay to apply yourself? Come along, three-thirty. . . . I'll die if you don't come soon.

The day passed somehow. For the life of her she couldn't have told what took place; she went from class to class in a sort of happy daze, hugging her secret to herself. What fun it would be afterwards when the news got around!

She paused at room 212 to get her breath. There was a little hum of voices inside. It sounded pleasant, and excitement mounted in her until she felt she would choke. She opened the door and walked in. They turned to her and her eyes ranged quickly over the gathering. . . . There was Miss Griscom, coming to meet her, and Mr. Hatch. Mr. Grauert, half hidden behind a movable blackboard, and Miss Haynes—that surprised her a bit—and oh, how nice, Miss Williams! But how queer Miss Williams looked. Though she nodded to Sue, she did not smile.

She greeted them individually, feeling that she was among friends, and sat down in the chair they brought forward. Miss Griscom made a pleasant little speech . . . phrases reached her, but try as she might, she could not connect them. "Of course you know why we have asked you to come . . . careful investigation and study of records . . . your outstanding ability . . . continuing scholarship . . . narrowed down to two girls . . . final decision, however, to award this substantial well-earned prize to you . . . one thousand dollars."

So it really was true. She was being told in plain words, even if the ringing in her ears prevented her from hearing all of them. She had heard the important ones, that was sure . . . 'to you . . . one thousand dollars.'

Their faces swam, their voices blurred. She seemed to be shaking all their hands at once. She heard her own voice, sounding stilted and queer and far-away, thanking them. "From the bottom of my heart," she said. "I feel so proud to have deserved this. It's going to mean so much to me."

They made a little ceremony of it. Miss Griscom handed the check to Mr. Grauert. Mr. Grauert handed it to her, with a nice little speech, too. "This will be sent to the paper, of course, and they will want your picture. We'll have a write-up in the State educational journals, and our school magazine is saving space for a write-up about the winner. We do congratulate you, Susan, on winning, particularly as the race was so close."

"Yes," said Miss Griscom, "we can tell you now that it was nip and tuck between you. The other girl's grades were a few points above yours, but all things considered—" She stopped in confusion, as if she was sorry she had said so much, and Mr. Grauert looked distinctly annoyed.

"It was the considered opinion of the committee, Miss Griscom, as you know, since we felt Susan could make better use of the money."

"But not all the committee, Mr. Grauert, was of the same opinion." That was Miss Williams speaking. Her voice was quiet, her face stern.

The roaring suddenly stopped in Susan's ears, and she felt cold all over. "I think I have a right to know who the other girl was—is," she said, "and what the averages were."

"Yes," said Miss Williams, "you have. Your average, Susan, was 96.5. Beth Varley's was 96.9."

"Then it was really Beth who won," Susan said slowly.

"The points were so very close," Miss Griscom hastened to cover up her faux pas, "that there was practically no difference, and we discussed it from all angles. We felt—"

"I'm sorry," Susan said, still in that slow voice. She looked around the room at the curious and intent faces. The prize had been hers for such a short time. It hadn't really been hers at all. "I couldn't accept it. It belongs to Beth."

How odd—how comforting—that it should be Beth. She had known all along of her scholastic standing. But they were in different classes; there was no way of actual comparison. If the prize could not be hers, she could not think of anyone she would rather have it go to than Beth. Beth could use it to even greater advantage than she. It was right and just.

They were all talking at once, angrily, sternly; expostulating, cajoling. Did she realize what she was doing? Did she know what this meant to the committee? Did she—

"Yes," she said. "I do know what I'm doing." She held out the check in its white envelope; the check she had not yet seen. "It's Beth's and it must go to her." She felt a kind of shame for them that they could have thought for a moment otherwise. When it had come to the final choice, between a Negro girl and herself, they had chosen her. Because she was not a Negro.

They knew what she was thinking. It was in her face, in her eyes that looked at them sorrowfully. She put the check into Mr. Grauert's hand. "She will make wonderful use of it," she said. And turned and walked out.

In the corridor she went along blindly, her mind still echoing with her own words. It was queer how she felt— not bereft or cheated or alone, but lifted up. And clean. As if a wind had blown around her and through her.

She heard her name being called, and called again. If they thought she would turn back or reconsider they were wrong. "Susan!" it came again, imperatively, and she recognized Miss Williams' voice.

"Wait for me." Miss Williams ran up and took her by the shoulders, whirling her around. "If nothing like this ever happens again in my teaching life, I'll still feel it was worthwhile," she said. She kissed Susan on both cheeks. "My dear, I'm so proud of you!"

Walking back from the baseball game with Dave in the soft spring twilight Susan caught sight of a vaguely familiar figure crossing the sidewalk in front of a group of stores, a bag of groceries up to her chin. There was something about her— "Oh," she cried in sudden recognition, "it's Miss Hamilton!" She started forward.

"Want me to catch her for you?"

Susan stopped short. "No—never mind," she said. Miss Hamilton had put the groceries in the front seat and gone around to get in the car. She had wanted to speak to her;

a strong, swift impulse to go up and thank her, to say—
But how could she have said it? It was so mixed up, Miss
Hamilton's words, remembered all these months, and her
own thoughts and actions. The poor dear wouldn't know
what she was talking about. . . . And yet maybe she
would. Yes, she *would* have understood. But maybe she
knows anyhow. Maybe she realizes what her words have
done to others and so she'd know how they helped me. I
hope she does know. I'd like her to.

While she stood, transfixed, the car moved off. "Lost
your chance," Dave said, tucking her arm in his. "But you
could always drop her a line, about whatever it was."

She told him what her impulse had been. "Isn't it
queer," she said. "I only heard her that once. I may never
see her again. And yet she influenced my life."

"Well, I don't know," David argued lazily. "She may
have set your purpose a little faster than it would have
set without her, but I'll bet you'd have acted as you did,
Miss Hamilton or no. That's the way you are." He stooped
down to peer into her face.

"Answer me straight out, Sue. Are you awfully disappointed about the way things turned out?"

She said honestly, "Well, I wouldn't be human if I
hadn't felt a good-sized twinge at what I was missing. But
that went almost right away. And I felt *good*. Just walking down the corridor that day I can remember thinking
things out way ahead. I said to myself, 'Suppose there'd
never been a prize? I can set my sights a little lower, and
maybe come out better at that.' I thought, 'Why, I could
go to N. J. C. instead. It's near home and I can commute

and save money that way. And their course is just as good.' "

"Good old Sue! It couldn't have influenced you any to know I was going to Rutgers right next door, I suppose?"

She said indignantly, "I didn't even know you were at the time!"

He grinned. "Calm down, firebrand, I was just trying to get a rise out of you. To my mind, the whole set-up's perfect. I may even get a jalopy of my own and tote you back and forth every day."

"That would be fun. . . . You know, Dave, I'm making it sound as if the going to college part was the most important, and it wasn't at all. It was what had happened to *me*. I'd had to meet a test, a big one, an awfully personal one. I had to make a real decision . . . it's easy to talk about what other people should do if and if so and so . . . but when it comes down to you it's different. Then you know whether you measure up or not. I'll admit I felt pretty rocky, as if I'd been tossed around in a storm. But I never had any doubts about what I had to say and do, and that's what made me glad."

"Me, too," he said.

"Beth's so happy. She's absolutely thrilled. It's going to make all the difference to her. Now she can go ahead. I'm as sure of it as I'm sure that we're walking along this street that she'll get where she wants to get . . . and this prize is going to boost her up the first couple of steps."

It was good to see Beth's happiness, to listen to her plans, to hear her joyful voice soaring in ecstasy morning and evening. She was going to Juilliard; she would have the best training; she would have sympathetic help and be launched, in time, under the finest auspices.

Oh, it wouldn't be easy. It was never easy for the artist, the Negro artist above all. Beth knew that and was prepared. But she would be on her way and she had the strength to see it through.

She had had her own kind of strength, Sue thought, and she, too, had seen it through. They both knew victory. But her own was of a peculiar kind.

David seemed to know just where her thoughts had taken her. He said, "Brookhaven High's not going to be the same kind of place any more. You changed it, and for the better."

"Oh, but David, such a very little! There's still a long way to go!"

"Sure; in the world, too. High school's a kind of little world. That's why it was important that we got started there, and we did. We started them down the right road, anyhow."

The right road. She remembered how, in the beginning, she had felt as if she must go down a road and the road was barred. So it had been. The bars had seemed insurmountable. But if you approached them right and were not afraid to work alone at first, you could take them away, one by one. Now the road stretched ahead, a better road for all of them.

"And things have been happening in the world, if you'll notice," David was going on. "That Negro appointed to the council in New York. That Negro educator down

South getting put into office, not just by the votes of his own people, but by a white plurality. Those things show how we're making progress. It's slow, yes, but until everybody—you and me and the rest—do what we can along the way, nothing gets done."

At least, she thought warmly, they had left their mark on Brookhaven High. And grown themselves in the process.

They had come abreast of the Varleys' house and their own. "There are the boys," Sue said. "Aren't they cute?"

Chuckles and Kenny ran to meet them. "We're building a treehouse," they panted in unison.

"In our maple tree," said Kenny.

"He's going to do the floor and I'm going to nail the walls," said Chuckles.

"Stu's good," Kenny said proudly. "He's keen with a hammer."

"We're going to live in it all summer," Chuckles announced.

"If we hurry we can get a coupla more boards up," Kenny said, and without further ado they ran back into the garden.

" 'A time shall come,' " Sue said, almost to herself, " 'when man to man shall be a friend and brother.' "

"And the time to start is like that, when they're young," Dave said. "Look, there's the new moon! Wish on it over your left shoulder."

She wheeled and wished silently. The wish brought the color to her cheeks.

When she turned back Dave leaned down and kissed

the tip of her nose. "Remember I said I was going to collect?" he reminded her.

Had he read her *mind*? "I thought you were never going to," she dimpled.

"That was it," he said. "You're a girl in a million, Sue. You're my girl, too, and don't ever forget it. I waited a long time so there'd be interest. And now I'm going to collect the interest." And he kissed her again very tenderly.